SILENCE

SILENCE

MECHTILD BORRMANN

TRANSLATED BY AUBREY BOTSFORD

amazon crossing

Text copyright © 2011 Pendragon Bielefeld

Translation copyright © 2015 Aubrey Botsford

Previously published as *Wer das Schweigen bricht* by Pendragon Bielefeld in Germany in 2011. Translated from German by Aubrey Botsford. First published in English by AmazonCrossing in 2015.

Published by AmazonCrossing, Seattle

www.apub.com

Amazon, the Amazon logo, and AmazonCrossing are trademarks of Amazon.com, Inc., or its affiliates.

ISBN-13: 9781477829097
ISBN-10: 1477829091

Cover design by M.S. Corley

Library of Congress Control Number: 2014920037

Printed in the United States of America

For Peter Gogolin

History: easy to think about, difficult to see for those who experience it in their own flesh.

Albert Camus (1913–1960)

Chapter 1

November 12, 1997

How quiet. Had it always been so quiet here? Robert Lubisch stood at the window and looked out over the garden.

At the far end of the extensive grounds, the tall Douglas firs glowed, almost blue, against a milky sky. Strands of early-morning mist lay on the lawn like cotton wool, shrouding the rhododendron bushes and the plinth of the life-sized marble Diana, frozen with her bow held up in a defensive pose. She had always been thus frozen; only occasionally, when the midday summer sun fell vertically on the garden, had the stone ever glowed warm and golden.

He still remembered the day she was placed there. Part of the fence had needed to be torn down so that the truck could come into the garden. He had been eleven or twelve years old. Her robe left her right breast uncovered, and in those first few weeks, anytime he felt unobserved, he used to climb up on the plinth and run his fingers over the perfectly sculpted nipple. The slight irregularities and the smooth, cool mound beneath his fingertips had aroused his first sexual fantasies.

He imagined Diana in his small garden in Hamburg, crammed into the space between the terrace and his neighbor's hedge. He smiled.

Too big. It was like that with everything he associated with his father. To him, Robert, everything had always seemed too big. The gestures, the house, the parties, the speeches, the demands, and the expectations.

Taking care of Diana would fall to the art and antiques dealer who had already begun to sell off the pictures, sculptures, books, and furniture. Perhaps the buyers of the house would like to keep her.

Robert Lubisch carried into the hall a box containing documents, his mother's jewelry box, and some books he did not want to part with. A few bubble-wrapped pictures and sculptures stood against the wall. These were the things he would be taking back to Hamburg.

The decision to sell the house had been a sober and logical one, but now it hurt. He had been close to his mother, who had died six years ago, but he had never lived up to his father's standards. And now, here in this gradually emptying house, he realized he no longer had to try; it was over. But he also realized—and here lay the pain—that he would now remain inadequate forever.

His gaze fell on the broad, mahogany-hued staircase that led from the hall up to the first floor. When he was a boy, the polished handrail had made a perfect slide.

This villa on the edge of Essen, between the Schellenberger Forest and Lake Baldeney, had been important to his father—a status symbol such as only a few could afford. Over the years, his parents had no doubt come to feel at home here, and his father had stayed on after his mother's death. Eight bedrooms and more than three thousand square feet.

He went back into the study.

Frau Winter, the housekeeper, who had run the house for thirty years, had found his father here ten days earlier. He had been sitting in his armchair, with his reading glasses on his nose and the newspaper in his lap. "He gave the impression of being busy," she had said on the telephone, in answer to his question as to whether he had died peacefully. "Quite busy, to the end."

The death announcement Robert had issued in the name of the family was lost among half- and full-page notices from the city council, the Association of Displaced Persons, and the Lubisch Corporation.

More than two hundred mourners came to pay their respects. The church choir sang "Unless a kernel of wheat falls to the ground and dies, it remains only a single seed," and three buglers played the "Last Post" at the graveside. The wreaths were piled so high, it was almost impossible to read the inscriptions. They came from the mayor, the planning department, the city council, various companies his father had worked with, the Association of Displaced Persons, to which he had given over part of his fortune while he was still alive, and, of course, the Lubisch Corporation, which he had sold five years earlier as Lubisch Inc. The Lubisch name had remained; the old man had insisted on it.

He ran his fingers over the highly polished walnut desktop. He had not come here much since his mother's death. Birthdays and the obligatory Easter and Christmas. His father had seen him as his successor in the construction business. When Robert decided to study medicine, he and his father had fallen out, and although they both avoided the subject in the years that followed, it had always stood between them; he heard the reproach in the old man's voice whenever the conversation turned to the company.

His father ran the firm until his seventy-fourth year, stubbornly clinging to the belief that his son would change his mind, that he might yet "see sense."

Robert Lubisch looked at his watch. The real estate agent was coming at nine o'clock with the first prospective buyers. If they wanted the house to be spick-and-span when they moved in, he would have to engage one of those house-clearance companies.

The term stung him; he felt coarse. What would remain of the great Friedhelm Lubisch? A company name and the symbols standing here in the hall, which he would pick up and hold in his hand in Hamburg from time to time.

He emptied out the desk drawers. At the bottom he found letters from his mother, carefully bundled together. He smiled. So his father had been like that too, the old mule. If he were still alive, he would vehemently deny this small show of sentimentality and probably claim he had kept them for his mother's sake.

Beside the letters, he found a cigar box made of dark, fine-grained wood. Incised into an oval of mother-of-pearl set in the center of the lid, a broad-hoofed horse dragged a covered wagon. The carved words, "Brazil 100 Percent Tobacco," had worn away. Inside, he found an SS identity card, a safe-conduct pass, and discharge papers for a prisoner of war. At the very bottom lay a sepia-tinted photograph with a serrated, yellowed border. It showed a young woman. The picture on the identity card was unrecognizable, but the signature read "Wilhelm Peters." The safe-conduct pass bore no name. Only the discharge papers showed his father's name.

Robert looked at the papers. The black spots on the identity card were caused by blood. His father had been from Silesia. An ordinary soldier, he had been taken prisoner just before the end of the war. But why did he have a stranger's papers?

He heard the real estate agent's car coming up the drive. He returned the documents to the cigar box, closed the lid, and tossed it into the cardboard box along with the photograph albums and files that he would sort out when he got home.

In Hamburg again that night, he put the box in the back corner of his study. It would be three months before he paid any further attention to it.

Chapter 2

February 18, 1998

Maren Lubisch was sitting in the living room that evening, hunched over one of the photo albums. Robert sat down beside her and looked with astonishment at the pictures of his father in his midforties. Maren laughed. "If I didn't know better, I'd say it was you." He had the same high forehead and prematurely gray hair, the same straight nose, and the narrow, somewhat severe mouth. From his mother's side he had inherited only his physique. Whereas his father was a rather hulking presence in the pictures, Robert had a much different build, his limbs being long and slender.

One photo showed them both in the study, behind the desk. Robert, age nine or ten, was on the armrest of the old mahogany chair, beside his father. They both looked surprised. Maren was about to turn the page when he put his hand between the pages and pulled the album closer.

In the photo, an open cigar box lay on the blotter.

"Wait."

He fetched the cigar box and placed it next to the album.

"Do you see that?" He pointed at the picture and felt the kind of unease that arises when something long forgotten takes shadowy form. He knew something about those papers.

He stroked the mother-of-pearl oval and opened the lid. The faint, sour-sweet scent of fine tobacco wafted toward him. The smell brought back memories. It was as if he could feel the pressure of the armrest on his buttocks and thighs as he pictured those few intimate moments he had had with his father.

"I deserted." He heard the old man's voice as if from a great distance.

He had been fighting with an armored division in the lower Rhine, and when the Allies' big offensive began and his two closest comrades fell down dead within minutes of each other, he lost his nerve.

Yes, he remembered it now.

His father had said, "I ran without thinking. Just away, away from the front. Away from all those dead men."

And one of those dead bodies had been SS Squad Leader Wilhelm Peters. His identity card was in his breast pocket, a folded sheet of paper with a photograph rendered unrecognizable by dried blood. In his coat pocket he found the safe-conduct pass, a small, linen-bound booklet. He removed the dead man's overcoat and tunic, appropriated the papers for himself, and, as SS Squad Leader Wilhelm Peters, managed to get through the German lines to the Ruhr. What he actually wanted to do was get home to Breslau, but people said the Russians were there and civilians were trekking long distances to get away from their homeland. In the Ruhr, he got rid of the coat and tunic and was taken prisoner under his real name, Friedhelm Lubisch. He was not released until 1948. He had tried to trace his parents and sister, and found out two years later, through the Red Cross, that they had stayed in Breslau and died there.

Robert Lubisch sat in silence for a long time.

He had gone into his father's study many times, in those days, and asked to hear the story. Over and over again. How close they had been.

Maren took the portrait of the woman out of the box. "What about the woman? Didn't he say anything about her?"

"No," said Robert, shaking his head. "He never showed me that picture, or if he did, I don't remember."

"Could it be your grandmother? Or an aunt?"

"Perhaps."

Maren turned the photograph over. On the back were the words "Photo Studio Heuer, Kranenburg."

"Look at this." She showed him the back of the picture. "Kranenburg's in the lower Rhine somewhere, isn't it? Maybe the picture was among this Peters person's papers. Maybe she was his girlfriend or his wife?"

They sat up late into the night, talking and speculating about who the woman might be, and the man too, this SS squad leader. Maren said, "SS squad leader" repeatedly; the "SS" hissed between her teeth, as if the letters had to be spat out. All at once the documents became important. Significant. Serious. The man was dead, perhaps the woman too. By turns, again and again, they reached for the photograph in which this woman smiled at them in an almost intimate manner. That was not how one smiled at a stranger. Not even at a photographer. Who was present? This Wilhelm Peters? Or Robert's father? After all, he had been there at the end of the war too.

Maren said, "Maybe she's still alive."

They did not say any more, and he did not make a decision. But it was working away inside him. Perhaps she really had been this Peters's girlfriend, but perhaps she had also been close to his father, so close that he had kept her picture all these years. But why had he never shown it, never mentioned the woman?

Perhaps his exalted father, the man above suspicion, had a secret after all. Robert liked this idea. Perhaps a weakness would be revealed, a small dent in the old man's smooth untouchability, against which he had struggled for so many years.

Robert smiled. It would be a kind of liberation for him to be able to cut his all-powerful father down to size. He wanted to know. Just for himself.

Chapter 3

April 20, 1998

Spring had followed hard upon a mild winter, and the thermometer had risen to a summerlike seventy-seven in recent days. The meadows of the lower Rhine were a rich green, sprinkled with the yellow of dandelions and the occasional long stalk and small pink flowers of lady's smock. The farms and villages looked as if they had been casually strewn across the plain by a huge hand, groups of houses cowering amid the flat expanse.

Robert Lubisch had been invited to a conference at Raboud University in Nimwegen, and he took the opportunity to investigate Photo Studio Heuer in Kranenburg.

Reaching the place late in the morning, he came upon a roundabout and then a street like a wide slash, on both sides of which the houses of dark red brick were thrust forward like front-row spectators. Small businesses and storefronts lay beneath steep roofs. Only a few people were about.

He parked his car in one of the bays at the side of the street and went into a pub with snow-white net curtains in the windows. The tables had heavy-duty, cream-colored tablecloths, and on them stood small porcelain vases with colorful plastic posies of the kind that could be kept clean with a feather duster. In a flowing hand, a slate by the counter advertised asparagus dishes. It was still early; the restaurant was empty.

A plump woman stood behind the counter, opening letters with a steak knife and casually discarding the empty envelopes into a wastepaper basket at her feet. An elderly man sat opposite her behind a half-full glass of beer, smoking unfiltered cigarettes. When Robert Lubisch took a stool at the bar, they both looked at him expectantly. He wished them a good morning.

"There won't be any food for another hour," said the woman. "At twelve."

He shook his head. "No, no. I didn't want to eat anything, thank you."

He ordered an espresso and took the portrait from the pocket of his linen jacket. "I wanted to ask," he began awkwardly, "whether you could maybe help me out."

He placed the photograph upside-down on the counter and pointed at the stamp. "I'm looking for this address. Photo Studio Heuer." He smiled with embarrassment. "It may not be there anymore, but . . ."

The woman, probably the owner, interrupted him. "Heuer, gosh yes, he's been gone at least twenty years."

The man leaned over the picture and nodded in agreement. "At least," he confirmed. He turned on his stool and pointed in no particular direction. "Used to be on the corner over there, where Linnen has his insurance office now."

"That's right." The woman was no longer paying any attention to her mail. "But before Linnen, it was Wiebke Steiner in there, with her children's clothes." She folded her arms and looked at Lubisch suspiciously. "Why do you want to know?"

He hesitated. For a moment he felt it would not be right simply to show them the woman in the picture. That was silly. He knew it. He turned the photo over. "Do you know who this woman is?"

The woman picked up the photo and examined it thoroughly. "Is she supposed to be from Kranenburg?"

Lubisch shrugged. "I don't know. All I know is that this photograph was taken at Photo Studio Heuer."

She handed the photo to the elderly man, who took it in his nicotine-stained fingers and scrutinized it at arm's length, frowning. He shrugged. "I'm not from around here. Didn't move here till 1962, and this picture is definitely older than that. But old man Heuer, he's still alive. Must be about ninety by now."

The woman was now openly curious. "What is it about this woman? I mean, why are you looking for her?"

Robert Lubisch lied, without really knowing why. A kind of unease was spreading through him. "My mother died recently, and this woman was her best friend when she was young. I happened to be in the area, and I thought maybe I could track her down," he said, a little too hastily.

The coffee machine let out a concluding hiss and gurgle. The woman placed his espresso in front of him.

"What's her name?" she asked after a lengthy pause during which she appeared to be considering whether she should believe this stranger.

"That I don't know, unfortunately."

She folded her arms beneath her ample bosom. "Hmm. Well, I'm not so sure either . . ." She scrutinized Robert Lubisch without embarrassment and then reached a decision. "But Heuer, he lives with his son in Nütterden." She reached back, opened a small door in the cabinet behind the bar, and took out a phone book. Licking her fingers repeatedly, she flicked rapidly through the thin pages.

"Here. Norbert Heuer. That's his son." She wrote the address and phone number on a waiter's pad, tore out the page, and handed it to Robert.

He gulped down his espresso, thanked her, and left a generous tip.

When he came out, the sun had brightened. He took off his jacket, laid it on the backseat of his car, and rolled up his sleeves. It was a long shot but, spurred on by his success at the first attempt, he decided to drive to Nütterden.

The single-family home, with its carefully tended front garden, was in a residential area that had probably been developed in the 1960s. As he got out of the car in front of number twenty-three, that same unease came over him again—the feeling that he was getting involved in things that did not concern him. He shook his head. What did Maren always call him? "My personal worrywart."

He rang the bell, and a woman of about sixty opened the white plastic door with the gold knocker, purely ornamental, in its center. He explained the purpose of his visit, and suddenly the whole thing felt unpleasant. What was he doing bothering people with photos that were at least fifty years old?

For a moment he hoped she would simply send him away. Then he would get into his car and take the most direct route to Nimwegen.

She said, "Well, you'll be lucky. If it's all so long ago . . . but come in and ask him yourself."

In the living room, a slight man was hunched over the newspaper with a magnifying glass. The furniture was brown and too heavy for the small room. The old man looked like a child in the big armchair.

He stood up with effort, and they shook hands. Robert towered over him by almost a foot and a half, and he sat down hurriedly. The old man's daughter-in-law offered coffee and then left the room.

Heuer looked up with large, watery eyes and waited. Robert thought about Heuer's profession as he looked through the viewfinder, waiting for the right moment, for that fraction of a second that was worth capturing. He leaned forward and pushed the photograph across the table.

"Perhaps you took this picture?" he asked quietly. "At any rate, it comes from your studio." He did not know why he was almost whispering.

Heuer picked up the magnifying glass and examined the front and back of the photo carefully. For a moment, Robert Lubisch glimpsed his watery eyes enlarged by the magnifying glass and was reminded of a lake over which mist gathers and never disperses.

"Yes, that's mine," the old man said, putting down the picture and magnifying glass. Robert had expected pride in his work, but his "Yes, that's mine" sounded resigned.

Frau Heuer came in with a tray, passed around coffee cups patterned with pink flowers, and poured coffee from a round-bellied pot with a matching pattern. Nobody spoke. Then she left the room again, and the soft emphasis with which she closed the door behind her gave this encounter an air of mystery.

The old man stirred his coffee, apparently listening to the bright and regular tone of the spoon striking the thin sides of the cup.

Robert waited.

"That's Therese," said Heuer, and he too spoke softly. His voice blended with the clinking of the porcelain, and to Robert it sounded as if he had sung the name. Heuer put his spoon to one side and looked up. "Therese Pohl. Later Therese Peters."

Robert shuffled forward a little in his chair. "Wife of Wilhelm Peters?"

"Yes," he said. "Wilhelm Peters."

Robert felt disappointment.

"Wilhelm went missing," said Heuer, taking a sip of coffee. "He's been missing ever since."

Robert frowned. "Wilhelm Peters has never been found?" he asked skeptically.

The old man shook his head slowly. "No. Never."

"Do you know, perhaps, whether Frau Peters is still alive and where I might find her? Or did they have children?"

He did not know why he was asking the question. In truth, his search ended here. He had not found some secret lover of his father's. But now the woman had a name, and it was as if she had come a little closer, stepping out of that sepia-hued distance.

Heuer picked up the photograph, and he seemed to be talking to the picture. "She went away too. Not long after . . . She was never heard from again. And . . . no, they had no children."

"Where did the Peterses live at the time?" asked Robert, trying to curb his increasing disappointment.

"The last place they lived was out of town." He gestured weakly with his arm. "In the Höver cottage."

He looked directly at Robert. "But tell me, how did you come to have the picture?"

Robert hesitated briefly, then decided on a half-truth. "It was among my father's papers."

For the first time, a smile appeared on the old man's face. "Yes, yes. Therese. That was one pretty girl. She wouldn't have stayed alone for long. Perhaps she found happiness after all."

As Robert was leaving, he stopped for a moment. He simply had to ask. "Herr Heuer, do you remember the photo session? Do you know whether Therese came alone, or with someone?"

The watery eyes shifted, and he stared ahead for several seconds. Then he shook his head. "No. I think she came alone, but it was a long time ago. I can't remember exactly."

Robert was standing at the garden fence with Heuer's daughter-in-law when he asked her the way to the Höver cottage. She told him. "But it was unoccupied until a few years ago," she said pensively. "It stood empty for nearly forty years. So I should think, if it's about such an old story, you'd be better off going directly to the Höver farm. Paul and Hanna Höver. They grew up here. They'll have a better idea, I'm sure."

Robert Lubisch thanked her.

The Höver farm lay beyond Kranenburg and looked well tended. A narrow asphalt drive led off the main road, past a tall hedge, and to the house. Behind it lay some whitewashed stable blocks. In the open barn stood an old tractor and two trailers. At the house itself, four wide steps led up to a heavy oak door. Terra-cotta pots overflowing with geraniums flanked the entrance.

Before he had even pressed the doorbell, a dog started barking inside the house. He rang twice, and the animal seemed to become more agitated at each ring; it was now yapping immediately behind the door. Robert took a step back.

There was no other sound to be heard. He looked around. There was a large empty space in the barn, beside the tractor, and he could see spots of grease on the floor. It seemed likely that a car was normally parked there.

He looked at his watch. He did not have much more time. There were horses grazing in a field next to the house, and there was a show-jumping area beside it; to the west, beyond the fields, a small house lurked alone in front of a copse of trees.

That had to be the Höver cottage. He could still try there.

Chapter 4

April 20, 1998

Rita Albers was transferring an oleander and two small orange trees into bigger pots on the terrace; the plants had spent the winter indoors.

Nine years before, immediately after her divorce, she had turned her back on Cologne and moved here. She had taken this cottage—in the middle of nowhere, as her friends said—on a lifetime lease. Her friends had also gloomily predicted that she would be lonely and would soon return. Instead, she had resigned from her job at a women's magazine and now worked as a freelance journalist. She liked coming back here after extended research trips to work on her articles in peace. She had never regretted her decision.

She was scrubbing the teak garden furniture with soap and water when the doorbell rang. She assumed it was the mail carrier and called out, "On the terrace."

When she looked up, she saw a stranger coming up the path into the garden. She put the bucket of soapy water on the table. "Can I help you?" she said in a slightly irritated tone, resting her gloved hands on the low balustrade of the terrace. She had put up a conspicuous sign bearing the words "Private Property" at the entrance. Cyclists and hikers were constantly taking a wrong turn here, mistaking her nature garden, with its large orchard at the back, for a tourist attraction and wandering in without so much as a by-your-leave. When she came home one day and found a group of cyclists having a picnic on the lawn, it was the last straw, and she put up the sign.

The man now approaching the terrace did not quite fit that picture. He was wearing neither hiking boots nor those body condoms plastered with advertising that cyclists wore.

"Forgive me for disturbing you. My name is Robert Lubisch." He stood at the entrance to the terrace, somewhat embarrassed. He cleared his throat. "Is this the Höver cottage?"

"Yes," she replied, a little less abruptly. She pulled off her rubber gloves and ran a hand through her short dark hair.

"I went to the Höver house, but there was nobody at home." He cleared his throat again. "In fact, I don't even know whether you can help me." He held up a small photograph. "It's about this woman. She used to live here."

Rita Albers's professional curiosity was aroused. "Come on up," she said impulsively. "It's time for a break anyway."

She slipped off her gardening shoes, held out her hand, and introduced herself. Then she led him into a bright, spacious kitchen. She maneuvered her slim body confidently around the heavy wooden table that stood in the middle of the room, surrounded by eight beige plastic chairs. She told him to sit down and placed glasses, a jug of orange juice, and a bottle of mineral water on the table. Once she had sat down too, she looked at him expectantly.

He laid the photograph on the table.

"This is Therese Peters," he explained, "and she probably lived here, with her husband, until the end of the war."

Rita Albers frowned critically and examined the picture. She looked at Robert. "That may be, but I didn't take this house until nine years ago. I mean, I don't quite understand what you want. Is she a relative of yours or something?"

Robert Lubisch shook his head. "She isn't a relative. I don't even know whether she's still alive." He thought for a moment: *What am I doing here? Therese Peters wasn't my father's lover. It's over and done with.*

He shook his head and stood up. "I'm sorry. Please excuse the intrusion."

Rita Albers looked at him, then stood up too.

"Now wait a minute. That's not right. First you make me curious, and then you just leave?" She smiled broadly. "I mean . . . I'm a journalist. Maybe I can help you."

Robert stopped by the kitchen door, undecided, and ran through her argument in his mind. A journalist probably did know how to proceed and would get information more quickly. Besides, she lived here; she knew the people. And if she didn't, that was all right too. In truth, the matter was resolved, as far as he was concerned, but now that the woman in the photograph had a name, it did interest him to know what had become of this Therese Peters.

He sat down and relayed what he had found out so far. Albers questioned him skillfully, and soon he was telling her about Heuer, Wilhelm Peters's papers, and the role they had played in his father's escape.

Rita Albers, sniffing a story she might be able to sell, offered to ask around a little.

"Do you have the papers with you?"

"In the car."

They sat without saying anything for a moment. In the garden, blue tits twittered in the silence.

"Look," said Rita, taking up where they had left off. "Now I'm interested too. After all, they lived here." She patted the table gently with the palm of her hand. "It must at least be possible to find out what has become of this woman."

She fell silent.

When he still seemed hesitant, she said, "You know, this house had been standing empty since 1951 or 1952—the Hövers didn't know exactly when. It was a real wreck. Smashed windows, holes in the roof, ruined furniture, garbage everywhere." She gave the table another gentle pat. "All I could salvage was this little treasure."

Robert examined the rough, sturdy table. Perhaps the Peterses had sat at this table, just as he was sitting with this woman now. The photo was taken in the early 1940s at the latest, so Therese Peters had to be about eighty by now. Perhaps it would mean something to her to hold this picture in her hands again.

He stood up and fetched the papers from the car.

He followed Rita Albers through a wide archway into a large room with sliding doors that opened onto the terrace. Twin sheets of glass on metal stands in the right-hand corner formed a kind of modern desk. The wall-mounted bookshelves reached all the way to the ceiling. The pale wooden floor, stripped and unfinished, gleamed almost golden in the fading sunlight.

Rita Albers scanned the photograph, the identity card, and the safe-conduct pass. The machine took several minutes. She printed out the photograph and gave the original back. A blurry black-and-white image gradually pushed its way out of the printer.

Robert looked at his watch. He had stayed more than an hour. They hurriedly exchanged business cards, and he drove off toward Nimwegen.

Rita forgot about the bucket of soapy water and the garden furniture. She powered up her laptop and launched an Internet search for Therese Peters. The German phone book had twenty-one entries.

The evening news was on by the time she hung up the telephone for the last time. She had contacted all but two Therese Peterses. None had ever lived in the Höver cottage, or even in Kranenburg, and she did not hold out much hope for the two she had not yet reached. The woman had not even been thirty when she left. She was bound to have remarried.

When Rita Albers went to bed, she decided to try the Hövers first, Hanna and her brother, Paul. They had probably still been children during the war, but they must have known the Peterses. The Hövers were hardly talkative people, and she did not maintain regular contact with either of them, but she had a good pretext. She was planning to dig a well, because piped water was so expensive. Paul Höver enjoyed talking about such things. He liked her garden too, and he was pleased when she asked his advice.

Chapter 5

April 21, 1998

She walked along the narrow track that linked the Höver cottage with the Höver farm. It was early, and the air was cool. A fine mist lay on the fields and pastures. The sun would suck it up bit by bit in the coming hours.

She could see Paul and Hanna in the horse pasture from a distance. He was busy with a bridle, and she was leading a white horse to the practice area. The Hövers ran a boarding stable. People came from far and wide to house their valuable horses here, and the local vets recommended the Höver farm whenever a horse needed to build up its strength gradually after an injury.

Paul's wife, Sofia had died of cancer. While she was ill, he had completely given up farming, from which they could make only a meager living anyway, and devoted himself entirely to her care. The farm had deteriorated significantly, and Rita was sure that Paul had signed the lease with her only because he was in financial difficulties. After Sofia's death, his sister, Hanna, who had been working as a nurse in Kleve, moved in. They refurbished and converted the stables, laid down the practice ground, and made good the barns and the house. Rumor had it that the money for all this had come from Sofia's life insurance.

Hanna had never married, and it was obvious at first sight that she and Paul were brother and sister. They were two big, strong figures, and Hanna, who, like her brother, wore rough overalls and checked shirts, was plump without looking fat.

Rita stopped by the fence and waved to them. They answered her greeting with brief nods and went back to their work. That was always their way. They would never stop working to say hello to her. Not to her, nor to the customers who drove up in their four-wheel-drives to drop off or pick up their horses. When it came to the Hövers, whoever you were, you waited until one of them had time for you.

At first, Rita had found their behavior arrogant, but she soon realized that it was not. They just had a very particular set of values. It seemed as if they followed a different clock. They would not interrupt a job in order to chat. Chatting was out of the question anyway. They were both friendly but reserved. They lived frugally, though they must have had a good income by now, and this frugality extended to the way they spoke.

It was a good ten minutes before Hanna led the horse from the practice ground back to its pasture, came to stand beside Rita, and said, "Morning." Then she waited. And that too was always her way. If people came to the farm, it was because they wanted something, so they should say what it was and then go away.

Rita felt for the copy of the photograph in her denim jacket. "Hanna, I have a couple of questions about the people who lived in the cottage until the end of the war. Their name was Peters, wasn't it?"

Hanna gave a short nod.

"It's about Therese Peters." Rita took the copy out of her pocket and handed it to her. "So, what I know is that her husband was killed in the war and was never found, and that she then went away too."

Hanna looked straight at her, unmoved, saying nothing. She barely glanced at the piece of paper. Rita swallowed. "It was Heuer, the photographer, who took the picture. Do you remember Photo Studio Heuer?" She cleared her throat. "At any rate, he said Therese Peters went away after that." Rita began to stammer, annoyed that she was losing her train of thought because of Hanna Höver and her infuriating coolness. She was quite unable to work out whether it was stupidity that lay behind that gaze or calm wisdom. She decided not to mention Robert Lubisch or his father's role in the story.

"And?" Hanna asked at last.

Paul came across the yard and greeted her with the same curt "Morning" as his sister.

Wordlessly, Hanna handed the piece of paper to her brother, and Rita thought she saw a brief twitch in the man's face. Surprise? Fear?

"I thought perhaps you might know what became of her? I mean . . . you must have known her."

The cawing of rooks and the sound of a car engine approaching and then receding built up in the silence that followed. A horse snorted in the pasture. Paul folded the photocopied sheet repeatedly into smaller and smaller rectangles, scoring the edges between his thumb and forefinger as if he wanted to cut it up.

"She went away," Hanna said finally, "and nobody knows where."

Rita, relieved that Hanna had said anything at all, immediately asked another question.

"Do you know when that was?"

"No." The reply was not unfriendly, but it came as blunt and direct as if Hanna had taken a potshot at her question with it.

"Her maiden name was Pohl, wasn't it? Did she have brothers and sisters who might be able to help me?"

"No." Once again, the reply was immediate and definitive.

Paul said, "You know, it was a long time ago. One day she just wasn't there anymore." He ran his hand through his unkempt, gray-brown hair. "Where did you get the photograph?"

Rita ignored the question. "The Pohls, were they from Kranenburg?"

Hanna shoved her hands into the pockets of her corduroy vest. "I have work to do," she said curtly, and went over to the stables.

Suspecting that Paul would soon leave her standing there too, Rita asked hastily, "And this Wilhelm Peters, was he from here too?"

He nodded.

Rita took a deep breath and forced herself to be patient. "And . . . did he have brothers and sisters, perhaps?"

"A sister."

"What about her? Does she still live here?"

"The war kept her."

The choice of words left Rita speechless for a moment. Kept by the war. Why would someone say that? Did it mean that, for the dead, the war was still on?

"But maybe you can—"

This time Paul interrupted her: "I asked you where you got the photograph." The firmness of his tone, coming from a man who was normally rather gentle, made her start.

It took her just a fraction of a second. "The old table," she said quickly. "You know I restored the old table. The picture was in the drawer."

Höver nodded. "Leave the dead in peace," he said almost comfortingly, then turned and headed back toward the pasture.

Rita Albers set off for home. It was not until she was almost at her front door that she realized Paul Höver had not given back the copy of the photograph.

Chapter 6

April 21, 1998, evening

After bringing the telephone conversation to an end, Therese Mende spent a long time on the spacious terrace of her house. Her eyes wandered sightlessly over the bay and out to the Mediterranean. The sea was calm. Some waves were breaking against the cliffs far below, while others continued into the bay and lapped up onto a narrow sandy beach where there were now more holidaymakers than a few days before. The tourist season was approaching fast, and peace would only return, gradually, in October. Shouts wafted up to her, fleeting wisps of words that vanished before giving up their meaning.

The calendar said late April, but this year everything seemed to be in a hurry. Summer's plays of light were already dancing on the water; soon the shadows of the cliffs would move across the bay like the hands of a clock and, at noon, that shadowless moment, converge.

Such urgency! With each passing year, the days seemed longer and the years shorter. Wasn't it only yesterday that the winter almond blossoms had been on the branches, glowing like pink snow?

Shaking her head, she turned away. A red-tiled roof, supported on four pillars of natural stone, extended the entire breadth of the house, plunging the terrace into shadow to half its depth. She went to the sideboard, took out the bottle of sherry and a glass, and sat down in one of the wide wicker chairs.

It was age. Time sped up with age. So one clung fearfully to every moment and hoped to see the next day too. A certain lack of moderation. A thirst for life that did not desire a longer life. A thirst for life that feared death.

She poured herself a generous glass and ran her left hand through her pageboy-style gray hair.

"The tenant," Hanna had said on the telephone. "The tenant has a photo and is sniffing around."

So that was how simple it sounded, when the past caught up with a person after nearly fifty years.

The sherry was dark and mild, leaving only a slight burning sensation on the tip of her tongue.

For the first moment or two, she had not understood what Hanna was talking about at all. In a way that was quite unplanned, the life of Therese Peters had receded over the years. Whenever she had filled in a form and entered Therese Mende, née Pohl, it was as if she were drawing a line through Therese Peters's life. The words piled up more and more densely over the images, and sometimes, in Rome and London, where she had spent the early years with her second husband, Tillmann Mende, she had stopped in the street and asked herself whether the seven years of being Therese Peters had really happened.

And now they were back, those drab and meaningless years, and she did not even feel surprise.

The woman claimed she had found the photo in the cottage, in the kitchen drawer, but that could not be right. Why did she say it? How had she really come by the picture? "A journalist," Hanna had said. Someone like that would go on digging. She would collect a whole suitcase full of verifiable facts, interpret them as she wished, and then talk in that arrogant way about truth. And none of it would be true.

Therese drank the rest of her sherry in one gulp and poured out some more.

All these years she had worked hard and, together with her husband Tillmann, built up the Mende Fashion label. It had not always been easy. Tillmann had a creative mind, but his recklessness had often brought them to the brink of ruin. It was not until he handed over the management of the business to her, and her alone, that things had started to go uphill. Today, Mende Fashion was a presence throughout Europe.

Tillmann's sudden death three years before had thrown her into a deep depression. Without his recklessness, at a stroke, nothing had any meaning; everything was pointless, empty. But she had not understood that until months later. She had handed the management of the company over to her daughter, Isabel, and retreated here.

Her husband was the only one who knew about her life as Therese Peters. Isabel had no idea.

She sat there motionless for a long time, her thoughts wandering aimlessly. The sun migrated inland. On the horizon, the line between sky and water grew indistinct. Soon it would disappear, and only the narrow band of spray where the waves broke would show that there was an above and a below.

Luisa, her housekeeper, was standing in the entrance to the living room, clearing her throat in that cautious manner of hers. Therese started.

"Excuse me, but dinner is ready," said Luisa, vanishing as silently as she had appeared.

Therese was not hungry, but she went in and made her way to the dining room. Her loose-fitting turquoise silk robe rustled at every step. She took only a few bites. As Luisa cleared the table, she looked at her with concern. "Didn't you like it? Should I bring you something else?"

Therese smiled and patted her hand. "The food is excellent, Luisa, but I'm not hungry today." The housekeeper's face relaxed. Deftly, she put the plates and cutlery on a tray and disappeared into the kitchen with it. A short while later, she came back one more time and said, as she did every evening, "I'll be going then, Frau Mende. Is there anything else you need?" and Therese replied, as she did every evening, "No, thanks, Luisa. Have a good night."

Then she was alone. With a woolen blanket around her shoulders and a glass of red wine in her hand, she sat out on the terrace again. The beach had emptied; the only sound was the constant, regular murmur of the sea.

Fragments of recollection came back to her, unchecked, swirling in her head like the remnants of a time that had collapsed in on itself.

Her mother kneeling among the pews, swathed in the bitter, musty scent of old incense.

Leonard, standing in the field of stubble and demanding her promise of eternal friendship, then later, his eyes wide with terror, impermanent as a ghost.

Yuri, who wanted to believe in God, pressing himself against the plank wall of the barn to stop himself from wavering.

Her father, with the eyeglasses in which one lens was shattered, wordlessly stroking her cheek with the back of his hand and trying to smile.

And Wilhelm. Wilhelm, pacing agitatedly up and down in her room and saying, at last, "Marry me."

The strangeness of the images soon fell away. The intervening years shrank to minutes.

Chapter 7

April 21, 1998

At about ten o'clock, Rita Albers rode her bicycle to Kranenburg. The red-brick facade of the town hall was almost completely overgrown by a wild grapevine. The young leaves lay against the masonry as if they had been waxed in place, glowing with the rich green of spring. The young woman at the residents' registration counter greeted her pleasantly. A plaque on her desk read, "You are being served by Frau Yvonne Jäckel." Frau Jäckel frowned with irritation when Rita introduced herself as a journalist and told her she was researching an old missing-persons case.

"Well, I don't really know. Such old dates. We have everything after 1950 in the computer, but before that . . ." She looked helplessly at Albers. "What were the names again?"

Rita smiled winningly. "Therese Peters, née Pohl, and Wilhelm Peters. If I've understood correctly, Wilhelm Peters was killed at the end of the war, and Therese left town shortly afterward."

The young woman shook her head. She entered the names into her computer, as if by force of habit, and Rita rolled her eyes.

"Look, the war ended in 1945. Do you have an archive, maybe? I mean, could I have a look?"

Frau Jäckel was fully occupied with her screen and asked, without looking up, "Do you have the birth dates?"

"Yes, Wilhelm Peters's." Rita took out the copy of the SS card. "Born June 22, 1920."

The young woman looked back and forth between the document and the screen. "I don't understand this," she said pensively. "I have Wilhelm Peters here, but he wasn't killed in the war. He was removed from the register in 1951, with the comment, 'missing.'"

Rita sat absolutely still for a moment. She asked, "Does it say when he went missing?"

The young woman turned the screen toward Rita. "Look here. Wilhelm Peters, born June 22, 1920, removed from the register March 18, 1951. And down here there's a comment: 'Reported missing August 15, 1950.'" She scrolled down a little. "And then here. Therese Peters, née Pohl, marriage certificate dated August 25, 1944. Likewise taken off the register March 18, 1951, this time with the comment, 'Moved to unknown destination.'"

Rita's thoughts came thick and fast. What was this? The journalist in her scented something. The story that Robert Lubisch had told her could not be true. Had he lied to her? Why would he do that? No, that was unlikely.

"What does that mean? I mean, why were they both taken off the register on March 18, 1951?"

Yvonne Jäckel leaned back in her chair, visibly pleased with herself and her database. "There's an official procedure. They wait a few months, try to find out where the woman has moved, or in case she deregisters in the proper way so that she can register somewhere else. As far as missing people are concerned, I don't have any personal experience, but I think the procedure is similar."

"Can you check for parents or siblings?"

The young woman tapped at her keyboard. When another visitor, a woman, came into the office, she hurriedly swiveled the screen back into its proper position and gave Rita Albers a brief, apologetic smile.

"I'll have another look later if I have time," she said, almost conspiratorially, "but I don't think I'll find anything here. The records of immediate relatives are linked, but I don't have any more entries here. If the people died first, or deregistered . . ." She shrugged helplessly. "You'd have to get in touch with the municipal archives, or ask at the church. The trouble is, Kranenburg was almost completely destroyed at the end of the war."

Rita pointed at the printer sitting on a filing cabinet behind Yvonne Jäckel. "Could you print out the data on Wilhelm and Therese Peters?"

Equipped with two further documents on the Peterses' life, she stepped out into the square. She pushed her bicycle down the main street and stopped at an ice-cream stand on an impulse. Four small tables had been put out on the cobblestones for the first time that year. The sun, pleasantly warm, still had the mildness of spring. She ordered a cappuccino and tried to bring some order to this new information.

Wilhelm Peters had not been killed in the war. Why had Friedhelm Lubisch served up this story to his son, and, above all, how had he really come by the papers? And if Wilhelm Peters didn't go missing until five years after the war, then it must be . . .

She finished her cappuccino hurriedly, paid, and rode out into Waldstrasse.

When she entered the police station, two officers were sitting at their desks behind a counter. A portly man in his late forties, with prematurely thinning hair, came over to her.

Rita introduced herself, took out the printouts from the residents' registration office, and laid them on the counter. She came straight to the point.

"I'm a journalist, you see, and I'm researching a missing-persons case from the year 1950. Wilhelm Peters is the name. He lived in the Höver cottage with his wife and was reported missing here in Kranenburg. His wife disappeared a few months later."

"The year 1950," said the man sonorously, having thoroughly examined the printouts in silence. He looked up and added laconically: "That's when I was born." He did not stir from the spot.

Rita took a deep breath. "Look, I'm not assuming you worked on the case back then. I'd just like to know where I can inspect the files."

The younger policeman at the desk seemed to be following the conversation with amusement.

"In the archives," said the fat one at length, in his rather ponderous way. "But first there would have to be a search, and that takes time."

"Oh, I'll wait." Rita smiled broadly. "I have time."

The younger policeman leaned over his desk to hide his grin. The older one examined her with his small brown eyes, as if she were some rare beast.

"You don't have that much time," he said, "or have you brought food with you?"

At this the man at the desk spluttered with laughter. This did not bother the fat one, who looked steadily at Rita as the other one left the room.

"Look, your archives can't be that big, and if they're arranged by year . . . I mean, I could help you."

"I see. You want to help," he said, again in his ponderous way, and Rita grew more and more annoyed. Was this fellow making fun of her joking, or was this just the way he was? And if he searched the way he spoke, then maybe the comment about food wasn't such a joke after all.

He glanced to his left across the counter and pointed at the clock hanging there. "Midday soon."

Rita was about to explode, when the young man came back in and said to his colleague, "They have them."

The fat one nodded with satisfaction. "You see? Order is half of life. We've investigated the matter." He stretched out the word *in-ves-ti-gat-ed*, emphasizing every syllable. "The archives are in Kleve, and the files are available."

Half an hour later, she swapped her bicycle for her runabout and drove to Kleve. They had been notified. She had to identify herself and was allowed to view the files marked "Disappearance of Wilhelm Peters."

Rita read and took notes.

Wilhelm Peters's wife reported him missing on Tuesday, August 15, 1950. They had been at the Marksmen's Fair in Kranenburg together on Saturday, August 12. Therese Peters had left the tent early; her husband had stayed behind. Since he usually made the most of such events by staying to the end, she had thought nothing of it when he did not come home on Sunday. She assumed he had been celebrating all night. It was not until Monday morning that she went back to the tent, expecting to find her husband having a morning drink. She did not find him, and she waited out the rest of the day. Wilhelm Peters worked in the planning department; he had taken Monday off and should have been back at work on Tuesday. As far as his job was concerned, he was reliable. On August 15, 1950, Therese Peters went to the town hall first thing in the morning and asked after her husband in the planning department. When she found out that he had not arrived at work, she reported him missing.

In the days that followed, the police established that Wilhelm Peters had not been seen since the Saturday night, and that some patrons had observed a heated altercation between him and his wife in front of the marquee. There were further reports that Wilhelm Peters had taken his leave, somewhat inebriated, after midnight. Soon it was being said that he was probably no longer alive, and Therese Peters came under suspicion.

Rita Albers looked up as a policeman brought her a cup of coffee.

"Oh, thank you," she said, smiling at him. "Tell me." Rita cleared her throat. "Your colleague in Kranenburg . . . Is he always like that?"

The man grinned broadly and nodded. "You mean Karl van den Boom? He's all right. He never loses his cool, and under the worst kind of stress he restores calm. He always says, 'If people would just do everything at half the speed, only half as much would happen.' We always send Karl out to domestics. As far as we're concerned, de-escalation has a name: Karl. And he has his own particular sense of humor."

"I'll say," Rita growled.

She leafed through the thin paper of the files, which rustled beneath her fingers, and found the record of the interview. Some of the typed characters seemed to have embedded themselves in the almost transparent pages over the years; they were pale and barely legible. The carbon paper had left halos around the lowercase *n*'s and *r*'s, and they lay scattered across the pages like small planets.

She pointed at the signature. "The reports are all signed by Sergeant Theo Gerhard. Is he still around?"

The man shrugged. "Certainly not in the police force, but he may still be alive. You'd best ask Karl." Rita groaned quietly to herself.

An hour later, having read the files, she snapped them shut. Therese Peters had remained the prime suspect to the end. She had been interviewed several times but had stuck to her story. There had been neither a body nor sufficient evidence.

Toward the end of the file were two handwritten notes.

Dec. 28, 1950

Frau Therese Peters did not comply with the summons of Dec. 21 of this year. Today, her home was found to have been abandoned. There were no personal items or clothing to be found. Her current place of residence is unknown.

Police Sergeant T. Gerhard

Feb. 15, 1951

Efforts to establish the whereabouts of Therese Peters have been unsuccessful. Since the circumstantial evidence against her in the case of the missing Wilhelm Peters has not been corroborated, we are abandoning the police search.

Police Sergeant T. Gerhard

Chapter 8

April 21, 1998

Therese Mende stared out at the moonless night, and the images rose up of their own accord from the blackness of the water.

At first she resisted, closing her eyes and trying to evade them. But random memories continued to dance, unchecked, beneath her eyelids. A keen, stabbing pain ran through her body, as fine as silk thread and cutting. She knew it, and she had felt it, along with a pounding heart, after her telephone conversation with Hanna. The period she had forgotten was breaking powerfully over her, crushing her with the weight of old images. In the distance, the orange lights of a containership proceeded slowly across the calm water, the only sign that time was not at a standstill, even now. So peaceful. So detached.

July 1939

For years, the six of them had been riding their bicycles the almost eight miles to school in Kleve together. The boys rode to Freiherr von Stein High School, the girls to the girls' secondary school.

Alwine, from the Kalder estate, had red curls and a loud, irreverent laugh, which she would let out over the schoolyard like a fanfare, and for which she was regularly entered in the discipline book.

Her older brother, Jacob, tall and thoughtful, carried himself with quiet pride. With his objective and self-critical manner, he even enjoyed the respect of the teachers.

Wilhelm, son of Peters, the pharmacist, faced all practical problems sturdily and energetically. He had risen to the rank of cadre unit leader in the Hitler Youth and worked hard at the difficult balancing act of overlooking his friends' critical remarks.

Hanna, the daughter of the Höver farm, had large ocean-blue eyes that looked out earnestly from above rosy cheeks. Hanna found book learning difficult and, at the age of fourteen, bore the responsibility for the household and her brothers and sisters after her mother's death.

Leonard, son of Kramer, the lawyer, was fine-boned and pale. He would pedal alongside Jacob and, when the wind was against them, put his hand on Jacob's back and push him. Leonard, the literature lover, could recite whole passages from Goethe's *The Sorrows of Young Werther* by heart.

And Therese, daughter of Pohl, the doctor, was seemingly in perpetual motion born of restless vivacity. Even in the classroom, when she was sitting quietly over her books, it was as if she wanted to reach out and grab the words and figures with her hands.

Their time together was due to end that summer of 1939. The boys had done their school-leaving exams, and the word *war* had established itself at every table in the community. In some houses it was whispered fearfully; in others it was spoken loudly and confidently.

Jacob and Leonard were to start their compulsory Reich Labor Service in a few weeks. After that they wanted to apply for officer training. In Jacob's case, this was a family tradition. His father, a colonel in the reserves, had already enlisted. Leonard had signed up against his parents' wishes. They feared for his health and had intended him to study law. Wilhelm would remain in Kranenburg and begin his training in the administration. SS Captain August Hollmann had said, "We can use you here, Peters. You'll soon make your mark."

Because of her poor grades, Alwine had to go to boarding school. "Alwine takes everything too lightly," the teacher had told her parents. "It's high time she grew up." Hanna left school that year, without a diploma, because both her older brothers had been conscripted and the work on the farm would never get done otherwise.

It was a Friday in August 1939. Wilhelm, responsible for the allocation of harvest duties within the Hitler Youth, had ensured that all six of them would be haymaking on the Kalder estate. They spent the whole day turning the hay in various fields. They laughed and joked, and the atmosphere grew more and more relaxed as midday approached. They exchanged playful remarks, and then the first hay began to fly. Competitions arose. Who would be the first to finish a row? The girls lost. Alwine sulked, complaining vociferously. Couples formed up, then switched. The day flew by. When they had finished, they did not want to return to the farmhouse just yet. Nobody said it, but there was silent agreement. They all knew this was the last time the group would be together in such relaxed circumstances. They sat in the field, talking and laughing boisterously. Glances were exchanged, eyes lowered in embarrassment, gestures interpreted. Hanna was in love with Jacob; it was an open secret. Alwine liked Wilhelm, and Wilhelm was attracted to Therese. There was a competitive edge to their banter, and when words flagged, guilty smiles hovered over the field of stubble, and the setting sun tinged the evening and their cheeks with red.

Wilhelm and Leonard talked enthusiastically about Germany's great future. Therese said, "Father thinks Hitler is rushing Germany toward disaster."

Birds were twittering in the forest; a dog barked on a distant farm. Jacob glanced at her briefly, and she thought she caught an almost imperceptible nod of his head. Wilhelm laughed. "God, Therese, your father was in the Center Party. He has to say that. But he's blind. With all due regard for friendship, he's been reported several times already, for things he's said. I think he should be a little more careful."

"But," she insisted, knowing herself to be safe among friends, "Father says Hitler is a warmonger."

Alwine looked at her with her large, imploring eyes. "Oh, Therese, do we really have to spoil this lovely day with something like that?"

Leonard jumped up. "Let's forget about politics. Today might be the last time we're all together, and I was going to suggest that we promise, here and now, never to lose sight of one another, and always to be there for the others, as we have been for the last few years."

It was not a solemn moment. They laughed with relief and the release of tension, and loudly sealed the promise.

The cheerfulness of the day had been like a finely spun thread. The arguments at dusk had almost snapped it. But they still managed the balancing act. They still knew how to place their friendship at the center of things and cling to it.

Therese Mende tried to call up a memory of the sky, of what it was like in those days. Had it really been as infinitely high as she now thought? So high that the naive optimism of six young people had found space beneath it? And a few weeks later, as she well knew, the sky had been a different one. When they said good-bye to Jacob and Leonard at the station early one morning, and the word *war* stood up from the tables and went on the march, the sky hung low and was like the inside of an oyster shell. In with the silver and steel gray, there shimmered antique rose and violet.

Chapter 9

April 21, 1998

In the afternoon, Rita Albers had tried to reach Robert Lubisch on his cell phone and, after the fifth unsuccessful attempt, left him a message on his voice mail. To distract herself, she went out into the vegetable garden and watered the rows of seeds and new growth. She carried the green watering can back and forth to the cellar door to fill it, and each round trip made her decision firmer. Once all the rows had been watered, she called Schoofs, the landscape gardeners, and requested a quote for a well.

After a cup of coffee in the kitchen, with her notes and the various photocopies spread out in front of her, she considered her next steps. She definitely had to get busy with the municipal archives. And she would talk to that Karl van den Boom again and find out about Sergeant Gerhard (retired). She should visit Heuer and perhaps . . . Pohl? The woman would have had to identify herself somewhere, to get work or lodging. Perhaps she had used her maiden name. She dialed the number of her journalist friend Köbler, who had a good track record of finding people. The word was that he had good contacts in the *Land* and federal police. They chatted about old times, and then she gave him an outline of the salient facts. Köbler promised to try. "Don't expect too much, Rita," he said at the end. "Much of the data from that time hasn't been digitized yet. If you're unlucky, the reports you're after are lying in some archive somewhere. You don't even have a location, and what if she's gone abroad?"

Rita shared his reservations. "But you'll try, won't you?" she pressed him.

Robert Lubisch did not call back until late that evening, when she was sitting at her computer, writing up the results of her research so far.

Rita told him what she had found out and heard his yesses and uh-huhs getting quieter and quieter, then finally disappearing altogether.

"Are you still there?" she asked when she had finished and she could not even hear him breathing.

"Yes," he said, and there was amazement in his voice, as if he did not believe his own yes.

Then she heard him ask quietly, "You mean, you think the man was still alive when my father took the papers?"

Rita considered this. She had not thought about it, but it was of course a possibility.

"Yes, that could be. It could also be that your father had something to do with Wilhelm Peters's disappearance."

"You must be mad!" Robert Lubisch exclaimed vehemently, and Rita thought she could sense his fear down the telephone line.

Then he collected himself and went on more calmly. "Frau Albers, that is a completely absurd suspicion. I consider it conceivable that my father didn't know the man was still alive, but . . ."

She heard him take a deep breath. "Listen, I don't want you to carry on with this. It was a stupid idea, and it's now clear that Frau Peters obviously began a new life. I'd ask you not to pursue the matter any further."

Rita smiled to herself. "Herr Lubisch," she answered coolly, "I'm interested in this story, and I'm not employed by you. I'm going to go on looking for Therese Peters. I'm an inquisitive person and, above all, I'm a journalist. A story might yet emerge from this, a story I can sell."

There was a pause. Then she heard a tight, "That's not fair, Frau Albers." He breathed hard several times before going on. "Please, let's talk about this. I'll be here in Nimwegen until tomorrow evening. I could drop by your house afterward."

She ignored his comment. "You know, I did a bit of digging on the Internet yesterday evening. Your late father, was he Friedhelm Lubisch, the building contractor from Essen?"

The call was abruptly cut off from the other end.

Rita looked at the telephone in astonishment. Then she reread the summary of her research. It was still quite meager. She added *Friedhelm Lubisch*, with a question mark.

"Not fair," Robert Lubisch had said, but what had he been expecting? Did he really think she would just go out and collect information on his behalf, out of the goodness of her heart? Besides, she had told him yesterday afternoon, in the kitchen, that the case interested her. She added her notes to the other files in the folder. He would calm down soon.

Chapter 10

April 21, 1998

Robert Lubisch sat in the hotel lobby, discussing the day's presentations with his colleagues, in English. Normally he had no difficulty following such conversations, but today he kept losing the thread, and on two occasions he even had to ask people to repeat questions addressed to him.

The telephone conversation with Rita Albers worried him more than he cared to admit, but at the same time he cursed himself for being an idiot. What had he been thinking when he left the copies with her?

Now it was definite: he could follow the conversation no longer. He made his excuses, went over to the bar, and ordered espresso and cognac.

It had been pure folly. All his curiosity about this Therese Peters was silly sentimentality, which he could no longer explain to himself. He had uncritically considered it a happy coincidence that he had come across a journalist, and now she could no longer be stopped. He felt like a traitor. What else would this woman bring to light? He took a sip of his cognac.

The idea that his father might have had something to do with this Wilhelm Peters's disappearance was absurd. He had been a prisoner of war until 1948; afterward, he had scraped a living as a laborer in the Ruhr. Besides, how could Peters have moved freely in the area, five years after the war, equipped only with an SS card and a safe-conduct pass?

No, the only thing his father could perhaps be reproached for was that he had not known Peters was still alive when he took his papers. Perhaps he had even known, but had taken them anyway.

The thought left him feeling faint. He sat down on a bar stool and drank his espresso. How matter-of-factly he thought this. How matter-of-factly he thought it possible of him.

He felt the heat of shame rising in him. What did he really know about his father?

He could list the facts, the things one put in a résumé. But he had never been close to Friedhelm Lubisch, the man.

When Robert was of kindergarten age, his father had been the hardworking man who would stroke his cheek with a callused hand that smelled of sweat and cement dust. He would take him to the bar after church on Sundays, where he would drink beer with other men in ill-fitting suits, argue, buy his son a lemonade.

When Robert started school, his father was busy setting up his own business. They would sit together at the breakfast table in the cramped kitchen every morning, and while his father drank coffee and smoked, he would ask about his grades, urge him to study hard, and look anxiously at his mother when he felt, again, that his son was not eating enough. On Sundays they would go to church together, and when the weather was fine, they would go for walks in the afternoon. His mother was wearing a camel-hair coat by then, and his father a wide-brimmed hat, which he would raise briefly when other walkers came toward them.

Just before he went to high school, they moved out of the small apartment in the center of Essen and into the villa on the edge of the city, and in that big house, it seemed to him today, they got lost. The big dining-room table alone, at which each person got a breakfast tray of his own because it would have been impossible to reach the butter without standing up, suddenly appeared to him, here in the hotel bar, symbolic.

"Now you have a big garden, all to yourself," he heard his mother saying enthusiastically, and the words "all to yourself" were still resonant. He sighed. Everything was too big, he thought, and he was glad the house had now been sold.

But it was precisely during that time, as they were moving apart at the speed of light, that there had been those moments of intimacy in the study, when his father had told him about his escape, about his fear. Sometimes his mother had knocked on the door and reminded both son and husband, in a way that almost expressed jealousy, that it was bedtime.

And now he had exposed those few moments of intimacy to a journalist. A wave of heat flowed through his body, and he did not know whether it was the cognac or the thought of his betrayal.

He felt a hand on his shoulder. His Dutch colleague and friend, Piet Noyen, praised his presentation that afternoon. They talked about the potential of gene technology in the treatment of tuberous sclerosis and the high hopes they had for it. This distracted him and restored the self-confidence he had lost in the last few hours.

It was past midnight by the time he showed his key to the man behind the counter and charged the drinks to his room. As he made his way to the elevator, his resolve stood firm. He would drive by Kranenburg again the following day and talk to Rita Albers. She would have to return the copies of the files. She had obtained them from him under false pretenses. She wanted to make money out of the story. So be it. He would buy them back.

Chapter 11

April 22, 1998

Therese Mende had had a restless night. As she tossed and turned in bed, it was as if an unseen hand were flinging more and more tiles from a mosaic at her, random fragments of a picture, and when at last she had fallen asleep, the life she thought she had forgotten still filled her dreams.

It was still early; Luisa would not come to work for another two hours. She went into the kitchen and made herself some tea. Bearing the teapot, cup, and milk jug precariously on a tray, she made her way to the end of the terrace and put the tray down on the little round table by the balustrade. Here, the cliffs plunged almost vertically downward, and one could be deceived into thinking one was directly over the water, as if on a wide diving board. It was still cool, and she pulled her thick white terry-cloth bathrobe tighter. It was going to be a clear, hot day. The curved outline of the sun was thrusting itself gradually upward on the horizon, rolling out a reddish, glittering, and ever-widening carpet over the sea.

What had any meaning? What had any meaning before today? The little things a person scarcely paid any attention to? Perhaps because one didn't pay attention to them, they collected like droplets in a bowl, spilled over the rim years later, and demanded the attention they had not been given before.

September 1939

Alwine was already at boarding school, and the war had begun, unreal and distant. Leonard and Jacob received their call-up to the Labor Service only a few days before they had to report for duty. Leonard ran to the Pohls' house, and Therese had hardly opened the door before he took her in his arms and whirled her around him. "We're going together!" he cried, overjoyed. "Jacob and I are going to Münster together!"

The morning of their departure was foggy, and the sky hung low. When Therese arrived at the station, after a ten-minute walk, she was late and soaked to the skin because of the clammy moisture penetrating the wool of her knitted jacket and her thick, braided hair.

Frau Kalder, Jacob's mother, was there, as was Herr Kramer, who was saying good-bye to his son, Leonard, and to Wilhelm. The train was ready to depart. She saw the two of them behind dirty panes of glass in one of the compartments and ran over. Jacob was heaving Leonard's suitcase onto the luggage rack. They were laughing. Jacob pulled the window down. He jokingly complained about the weight of Leonard's suitcase and promised to write. Leonard blew kisses at her. She held up a bundle containing a carefully packed apple cake she had baked the night before. The train moved off, and the two young men leaned out of the window. Leonard called out, "See you at Christmas."

Their heads and their waving arms disappeared into the fog, like a pencil drawing being rubbed out, line by line, by a dissatisfied artist.

When she came out of the station, Frau Kalder had already left. Herr Kramer was standing next to his car, with Wilhelm. She went over to them and heard Kramer thank Wilhelm. When he saw her, he climbed hastily into the car and drove off. Wilhelm came over to her and smiled. He said, "And then there were three."

"Yes, but where's Hanna?" she asked, surprised.

"She said good-bye yesterday evening. She has to help with the milking in the morning, she says, but I think she's a little jealous of Leonard. After all, he's going to have Jacob by his side every day." He laughed.

He had come by bicycle, and he gave her a ride back on the crossbar. She sat between his arms and felt his tobacco breath on her neck.

"What was Herr Kramer thanking you for?" she asked as the damp fog gathered in fine pearls of water in her hair. Wilhelm's head was immediately behind hers.

"I did him a favor."

"What favor?"

Wilhelm said nothing for a moment. Then he said, "But you're not allowed to say anything about it, promise?"

She nodded.

"Leonard was actually supposed to do his labor service in Hannover. Old man Kramer asked if I could arrange for Leo to be with Jacob and not so far away . . . and, well, through Hollmann, I was able to do something."

There was both embarrassment and pride in his voice. Therese laid her hand on his arm and cried out happily, "You're a sweetie, Wilhelm. Someone who can be relied on."

He asked her to come to the Jägerkrug pub with him that evening, and she accepted his invitation.

That day, for the first time, she thought about the many things she now had to keep quiet about.

A few days before, her mother had asked her to be careful with Tönning, the shoemaker, and his mother, Thea. She was not to tell them that her father was often absent at night. Her parents had been friendly with the Tönnings for as long as she could remember. Her father had treated the shoemaker's stump for months, without charging him, and Thea Tönning had been in and out every day when Therese's mother lay ill with diphtheria.

What if Father, with his firm rejection of the National Socialists, was wrong? She heard it on the radio, saw it in the weekly newsreel, and read it in the newspaper. Its rise was there to be seen and felt, every day. Everyone was joining, and she was standing to one side, although in truth she wanted to belong.

That afternoon she went over to the fabric and dry-goods store to buy some clothes-pegs for her mother. The owner, Gerda Hoffmann, was active in the National Socialist Women's League; in the window she had a display of Hitler Youth braids, epaulettes, and cords, as well as a mannequin dressed in a League of German Girls uniform. There was a sign hanging on the door: "Flags Sewn in All Sizes."

When Therese entered the store, Frau Hoffmann and Frau Reichert, the baker's wife, broke off their conversation immediately. Frau Hoffmann asked pleasantly, "Therese, I hear you're still not a member of the League." She shook her head uncomprehendingly. "I'd consider it. It doesn't look good not to be." Lips pursed, she fixed Therese with a stare, as if scolding a naughty child. Frau Reichert pretended to be absorbed in some edging fabric.

Therese did not immediately know how to answer; she felt only that the truth, namely that her father was strictly against it, would not be wise.

"I have so little time," she said hurriedly. "School. And Mother can't do as much, so Father needs me in his practice."

But Frau Hoffmann would not let go. "That's all well and good, but if that's the only reason, you could still come to the events. It would do your whole family good." She smiled. Her tone hovered between encouragement and threat.

"I'm going away to study after my diploma. I thought it would be best if I joined the Students' League," she said, proud of this stroke of inspiration.

Frau Hoffmann looked at her skeptically. "Oh, the little miss wants to go to university. I hardly think they'll accept you. I'm sure there are enough people who have already proved their loyalty to the fatherland."

Therese swallowed hard. In order to bring the conversation to an end, she said, "All right, I'll come on Monday evening and become a member."

When Wilhelm picked her up to go to the Jägerkrug, she was glad her father was not yet home and she had not had to confess her promise to Frau Hoffmann.

Many of the customers in the Krug were in uniform. Wilhelm offered her his arm and led her straight to SS Captain Hollmann's table. The captain stood up and greeted her gallantly. Wilhelm was about to introduce her when Hollmann said, "Not necessary. Fräulein Pohl is well-known to me." Then he ordered loudly, "A chair for Fräulein Pohl!" Therese was unsettled. How did Hollmann know her? She had never had anything to do with him.

The chair was brought, and she was forced to sit beside him.

"What will you have, mein Fräulein? It's on me, with pleasure." Therese glanced uncertainly at Wilhelm. She did not know how to behave, and she could only think, *Be careful! Be careful! Don't say the wrong thing!*

Wilhelm nodded at her, the way one nods at a child to encourage him to try something new.

She asked for a glass of white wine. When the drinks were served, Hollmann took up his glass and offered a toast. He said, "I'm impressed, and I know the value of what you've done."

Therese thought Frau Hoffmann had talked to him, and he was referring to her promise to join the League of German Girls. She was surprised at the little things he evidently took an interest in. For a moment she felt good. From Monday on, she would belong. From Monday on, everything would be easier.

Hollmann talked some more. She could hear the self-satisfaction in his voice. They clinked glasses. Hollmann's words blended with the bright, rising note made by the glasses as they touched.

To the present day, Therese's recollection was that it was not Hollmann's words, nor even his voice, that had suddenly made her afraid. It was the soft, rising melody of the glasses. It was the dissonance between the voice and the floating sound. Without any particular reason for it, she knew that Hollmann was talking about something else. She fell silent. Waited. Looked inquiringly at Wilhelm and spun the stem of her glass in her hand. Hollmann laid his hand on her upper arm. Then he said, "You're doing the right thing. Precisely because he's your father. Maybe being arrested will bring him to his senses."

She remembered a sequence of pictures. Pictures without sound.

The wine spilling onto the wooden floorboards and dripping unhurriedly into the cracks between the planks. And a small feather. Some winter down from a hen or a duck. It was on the floor. The draft from the falling glass sent it up in the air. Only briefly. Then it dropped back into the spilt wine and drowned, still dancing.

She heard Luisa crossing the terrace. "Good morning, Frau Mende," she said in her hesitant way, as though asking whether she was intruding.

"Would you like to have breakfast outdoors?"

"Good morning, Luisa." Therese looked at her watch in irritation. Yes, it was eight o'clock already. She stood up, somewhat embarrassed. She had never received her housekeeper in her bathrobe before. What would she think of her? "Please forgive me, Luisa. I lost track of the time. I'll get myself ready first and have breakfast later."

Chapter 12

April 22, 1998

Rita Albers called the municipal archives early the following morning and was given an eleven o'clock appointment with Herr Scholten. A rather young man welcomed her with a short, stiff bow and led her to a room dominated by a large conference table. "I've assembled some files, on the basis of the information you provided on the telephone." His speech was stilted, the words cleanly articulated; he pointed at some papers laid out neatly on the table.

Rita found Therese Pohl's certificates of birth and baptism. Margarete Pohl, Therese's mother, had died in 1944; her father, Siegmund Pohl, in 1946, after the end of the war. At first, the family had lived in the town. Siegmund Pohl had had his practice there. Then, in 1940, they had moved to the Höver cottage. There was nothing in the files to indicate whether he had continued to practice as a doctor.

"And Wilhelm Peters? Is there anything on Wilhelm Peters?" asked Rita, having noted everything down.

The man indicated another file with a small gesture. "Perhaps you'd like to have a look at that." He watched every movement of Rita's hands, as if worried she might handle the documents improperly.

Wilhelm Peters, born 1920, son of Gustav Peters, the pharmacist, and his wife, Erna. Parents' residence transferred to a new address in Schwerte in 1946.

Rita wrote this information down too.

"Wilhelm Peters was in the SS. Don't you have anything on that?"

The man leaned forward and, frowning critically, sorted the now-jumbled papers. "We do have a problem, in that we have hardly any files from the National Socialist period. Much was consumed by fire when Kranenburg was flattened, but we have to assume that most of it was deliberately destroyed so that it wouldn't fall into the hands of the occupying forces." He pursed his lips and shook his head, apparently seeing this act as a personal affront.

"What we do know is that Peters was investigated in the process of de-Nazification and categorized as a follower. As far as Dr. Siegmund Pohl is concerned, we know he was a local councilor for the Center Party until 1933 and a declared opponent of the National Socialist Party. An exchange of letters between the pastor at the time and his bishop mentions that Pohl was arrested and forced to give up his medical practice. He and his wife seem to have had very close ties to the Catholic Church. He was repeatedly accused of subversion in word and deed."

"Oh!" Rita scratched her head with the end of the ballpoint pen. "Well, that's certainly interesting. And the daughter marries an SS squad leader. Old Pohl must have been delighted."

The archivist raised an eyebrow reproachfully but said nothing. He stood up and organized the papers back into their folders and binders. As he was clipping Therese's birth certificate back into place, he paused. He took it out again.

"Did you see this here?" he asked Rita, indicating a penciled note on the back.

Certified copy issued Sept. 18, 1952.

Rita stared at the piece of paper. "Is there an address? I mean, was it sent somewhere? If so, there must be an address." Her voice almost cracked with excitement.

Herr Scholten flipped expertly through the binder again. "No," he said at last. "No correspondence. So we have to assume the copy was picked up from here."

"Shit!" she blurted out. "That would have been too good."

Scholten started and cleared his throat. He heaped the binders onto a wheeled cart and pushed another two folders toward Rita. "As far as your request about the missing Wilhelm Peters is concerned, I can show you a few articles from our newspaper archives. However, I haven't found anything about the disappearance of Therese Peters." As she began to leaf through them, he reached out with his index finger and tapped some colored paper clips he had used to mark the relevant pages. "You may wish to turn to these."

There were three articles. The first, written a week after Peters's disappearance, was no more than a kind of request for anyone with knowledge of Wilhelm Peters's whereabouts to report to the local police.

The second, four weeks later, already implied unambiguously that Wilhelm Peters must be presumed dead. Though there were no direct allegations against Therese, there was nevertheless the following sentence: "The police doubt his wife's statement."

The third and last article had appeared in December, its headline reading, "Still No Trace of Wilhelm Peters." This article did not reveal anything new to Rita Albers either.

Scholten expertly returned the folders to the cart, and then escorted Rita to the door. She thanked him and held out her hand to say good-bye. His handshake was unexpectedly firm and dry.

On her way home, she wondered why the police had closed the file after only two months.

Once home, she immediately picked up the telephone and called her colleague Köbler in Cologne again. "I haven't got anywhere yet," he said as soon as she identified herself.

"That's not why I'm calling," she replied. "I have some additional information." She told him about the copy of the birth certificate. "She must have used it to get papers. Maybe you could concentrate on the period at the end of 1952."

Finally, she tracked down retired police sergeant Gerhard. He lived in Kleve. He remained silent at the other end of the line for a long time after she had explained her request. "Come and see me," he said at length, in a heavy, scratchy voice, and they arranged to meet the following day.

She was standing in the kitchen, making herself some coffee, when Köbler called back.

"Tell me, what's it really about, this thing with Therese Pohl?" he asked without preamble.

"Do you have something?" she cried excitedly.

"Maybe," he replied cautiously.

Rita immediately knew he had something, and that, if he was trying to pry information out of her first, it was not trivial. She would have to show she was willing to meet him halfway.

"I found an old photo here in my house. Pohl lived here after the war, and I wanted to know what had become of her."

Köbler burst out laughing. "Come on, Rita. I'm not an idiot. There's a story behind this."

Rita thought quickly. "I don't know," she said at last, "but there could be. I still have too little."

There was a short pause. Then Köbler said, "Okay, so there's no such person as Therese Peters, née Pohl. There's only a Therese Pohl, from Kranenburg, who registered in Frankfurt from 1952 on and worked as a seamstress."

"But . . . how come the police didn't find that out at the time?"

There was a short laugh at the other end of the line. "They weren't as connected up as they are now. Besides, I assume they were looking for Therese Peters."

Rita thought about the police having given up the search after only two months.

The silence at the other end of the line told her Köbler had not yet finished. She collected herself and granted her old friend his moment of triumph, one she knew well herself—the moment one knew one had discovered something decisive.

"Listen, will you cut me in if you sell the story well?"

She hesitated. "Yes, fine by me."

"Shall we say twenty percent?"

Rita swallowed audibly. She knew the information was worth something if he was making demands like this.

"Ten," she countered.

His silence made her nervous.

At last he spoke again. "Okay, ten. So, this Therese Pohl married again in 1956. So, if your information is correct, we're talking bigamy, right?"

She was momentarily disappointed. "Oh, for goodness' sake," she said weakly. "Nobody will give a damn about that anymore, especially as Wilhelm Peters was registered as missing and the marriage could have been annulled easily."

And then he said, "Yes, yes, that's right, but Therese Pohl didn't marry just anyone. She married . . . Tillmann Mende."

It took Rita several seconds to place the name. "Mende? You mean Mende Fashion?"

"Exactly. Therese Pohl, or Peters, or whatever, is now Therese Mende and one of the most successful businesswomen in the country."

Rita's thoughts came thick and fast. Her hunch had been right. This *was* a story.

"Do you happen to know—"

He interrupted her. "She retired from the business three years ago and now lives in Mallorca."

"Where in Mallorca?" she asked breathlessly, scribbling *Mende* and *Mall* in a notebook.

"We're still talking ten percent, as agreed? It wasn't easy to find her address, I can tell you."

"Of course. Promise," she confirmed impatiently.

He gave her the address.

"Keep me up to date," he added.

After she had hung up, she sat quite still for several minutes.

Then she jumped up, pulled the telephone cable out of the socket, plugged in the Internet connection, and keyed in "Mende Fashion."

Chapter 13

April 22, 1998

Luisa cleared the breakfast table, and Therese, wearing a blue taffeta caftan with matching slim-cut trousers, set off on her daily walk around the bay. The street led steeply downhill past several small hotels, cafés with views, a real estate agent's office, and a tourist shop. She exchanged a few words in Spanish with the owner of the shop, who was dragging racks of beach toys and postcards out onto the street and complained about the slow start to the season.

The sandy beach was only five hundred yards wide, but there were narrow paths cut into the cliffs to the right and left, and it was possible to walk out at either end and skirt several bays along the water's edge.

A light breeze had sprung up, and out on the windsurfing school's platform, beginners in wet suits were struggling with boards and sails. She could hear their shouts and laughter and the rhythmic pounding of the waves. This lightheartedness.

Autumn and winter 1939

The following day Therese had gone to the town hall and asked to see her father.

Herr Grünwald, the policeman, whom she had known since she was a little girl, shook his head as soon as he saw her. He walked her to the door and said, "I'm so sorry, Therese, but there's nothing I can do. Your father's in Kleve." He was about to stroke her cheek, as he used to, but his arm dropped. "It will all be cleared up," he whispered. "The pastor's already been, and I heard Colonel Kalder called. I'm sure they'll release him soon."

On the third day, she waited for Wilhelm in front of the town hall.

She saw his shock, felt shame mounting in her head and her face turning red. He said good-bye on the steps to two men in SS uniforms, crossed the square, and signaled with a jerk of his head that she should follow him.

She waited a moment before entering the alleyway he had disappeared into. Suddenly, a hand pulled her into an archway that led to a courtyard behind a pair of houses.

"I'm sorry, Therese. You have to believe me. I didn't know anything about the arrest. I would never have taken you into the Krug with me if I'd known." His voice was pleading, and Therese was surprised. The idea that Wilhelm might have known about her father's arrest that evening had not even entered her head.

"That's not what I think, Wilhelm. Tell me, how is he? Where is he? What is he accused of?"

Wilhelm went on talking, but he had not heard her questions. "Therese, we can't meet so publicly anymore. You have to understand. Your father has caused us the worst kind of problems, and that evening . . ." He did not look at her. His gaze wandered searchingly over the gray facade of the courtyard wall, pausing on the small darkened windows as if trying to make out silhouettes.

"You shouldn't have just run away. Can you see that? You made yourself look suspicious. Yourself and me. They questioned me really thoroughly."

"I'm sorry, Wilhelm. I certainly didn't mean to get you into trouble."

He waited a moment, pensive. Then he said, "Your father's a collaborator, do you understand? They suspect him, together with others, of having smuggled communists and Jews across the border into Holland."

Therese swallowed hard. She felt the fear in her belly first—a hard chill, like steel, that spread out and slowed her thoughts. Her father's all-night absences, explained away as house calls by her mother, which she was not supposed to mention to anyone. "Please, Wilhelm, have you seen him? How is he?" Tears were running down her face, and she felt the trembling of her voice in her throat.

He grabbed her by the arm. "I haven't seen him, but I've heard he's not talking. They're interrogating him. He has influential advocates— I'm sure they'll release him soon." He took her face between his hands and looked at her intently. "Therese, you have to distance yourself from your father. Join the League. Participate. Hollmann thinks if you don't show that you . . . which side you're on . . . Do it for my sake, please." Then he kissed her on the mouth. When he noticed that she did not return his kiss, he took a step back and looked at her penetratingly. "I love you, Therese. Do it for us."

Her body felt stiff and unmoving; her thoughts were sluggish, and she could not think them through to a conclusion.

Wilhelm loves me, she thought, searching for some kind of sensation in her wooden body, a feeling that went beyond friendship. A moment of happiness, perhaps, a moment of sincere attraction that demanded a greater closeness. But instead, she wondered why he was making this declaration now, in the secrecy of a courtyard, hurriedly and in a whisper.

And she thought about Alwine, who was in love with Wilhelm and was her best friend.

She lowered her head. "Wilhelm, I need to think." She stepped hastily out from the archway and into the alley. "Mother will be worried," she whispered, and walked away at a quickened pace.

Anxiety and loneliness tormented the following days. She did not go to the town hall again.

Later, she had often thought about the distance that appeared between two people when love was the subject and that love was one-sided.

In the evenings that followed, she stood by the living-room window and watched Wilhelm on his way home from the town hall. His path led past her house, and he always looked up. She waited in vain for the impulse to run out, throw herself in his arms, and say, You're right. I'm confused, and I make things unnecessarily complicated.

Then she would turn away and look over at her mother, who was mending clothes with trembling hands. Her mother did not leave the house anymore.

At night, Margarete Pohl now sat quietly at the kitchen table, gazing out at the darkness beyond the window. She did her daily chores mechanically, often pausing suddenly and staring ahead. Then, as if awakened, she would look around the room in surprise, as if the place were unfamiliar. Her nervousness had left her, and it sometimes seemed to Therese that her mother was glad at least to know where her husband was. Indeed, she had the impression that her mother thought prison was a place of safety for her father.

It was early on a Monday morning. The sun had lost some of its strength, but the days were clear and bright. The trees and hedgerows displayed the reds and golds of fall, and the sweet scent of late-season apples and pears mingled with the earthy smell of freshly plowed, winter-ready fields.

Therese was helping her mother with the laundry. She came out of the cellar with a wicker basket full of boiled linens and put it down in the yard. She used a rag to wipe the lines that were stretched out over five poles. She had tied the little bag of wooden clothes-pegs like an apron in front of her belly. The cold bit into her wet hands as she hung a wet sheet over the line. At that moment she saw him, standing by the back gate to the yard, and she cried out.

He had a gash over his right eyebrow, his left eye was swollen shut, his lips split open. Margarete Pohl came running up the cellar steps and stared at her husband. Then she clasped him in her arms, whimpering, "It's not true. It can't be true."

Over and over again she touched his battered face. Over and over again she repeated the same phrase. Her father was weeping. Therese had never seen her father weep. Her mother pushed him into a chair in the kitchen, poured hot water from the kettle, wiped the crusted blood off his face.

Therese sat down beside him. He reached for her hand. Once her mother had treated the wounds, she took off his shirt and jacket. She staggered back and dropped heavily onto the kitchen bench. His trunk was covered with bruises.

Therese Mende remembered the silence. The kind of silence in which one breathlessly seeks words one does not know. Which one has to invent.

"Those will heal," said her father, as if there were other things besides, things that would never heal.

Her mother put him to bed. When she came back down, she went at things with more strength, sweeping the kitchen with short, angry strokes of the broom. She, who went through life gently, almost lethargically, now seemed to have summoned up all her reserves. She went up to the bedroom repeatedly, as if to confirm that he really was lying there and that they really had dared to strike him. It was as if she could not believe that, outside, this day was continuing like any other.

That night, Therese was awakened by a sound in her bedroom. When she opened her eyes, her father was sitting on the edge of the bed. He put his finger to his split lips.

"Therese, I know it's asking a lot, but you have to do something for me."

She sat up. He undid a ribbon that was wrapped around a sort of leather wallet. She recognized identity papers.

"These things have to go, urgently, to the lookout tower behind the Kalder estate. Do you remember it? We used to go there sometimes. The clearing, not far from the Dutch border."

She nodded. Wilhelm's voice danced through her head. *Collaborator . . . He stands accused of treason.*

She had walked past the lookout a few months before, with her friends. "Yes. But it's a ruin. There's . . ." Her father put his finger to his lips again.

"The wall on the left-hand side is made of a double thickness of planks. The middle one is loose. You must take it out and push the folder into the gap. Make sure it sits firmly and can't slide down."

Therese nodded again automatically.

"Go to the Kalders' first, mind. Whatever you do, don't go straight to the tower."

Siegmund Pohl opened the drawer in her bedside table and placed the leather wallet inside.

She risked another whispered question. "Who are those papers for?"

He leaned forward. "For people who must urgently leave this country."

He kissed her on the forehead and stood up with effort. She pulled him back by the hand.

"They say you're a collaborator."

Siegmund Pohl looked at her seriously. "I'm a Christian, Therese. A Christian and a democrat."

Once her father had left, she took out the leather wallet and opened it. Van de Kerk. Henk van de Kerk, Sophie van de Kerk, and their children Hendrika and Jan. And a young woman, not much older than her. Leni Platjes.

Therese swallowed. She knew the woman. She wasn't Leni Platjes. She was Karla Goldbach, who had done her final exams at her school two years before.

Years later, Therese Mende had told her husband that she made a decision that night. That seemed smug now. She had not made a decision. She had wanted to do her battered father this favor. That was all.

The next day, immediately after breakfast, she took her bicycle and rode to the Kalder estate. When she arrived, she asked whether Alwine would be coming home that weekend, and whether they had heard from Jacob. She was given a large cup of hot coffee in the kitchen, and Martha, the maid, related the latest gossip. Nobody mentioned her father, though she was sure they all knew about his arrest. Old Martha patted her on the head as she set off. The leaves of the blackberry bushes along the track glowed in tones of fuchsia and terra-cotta, and when she reached the forest path, the light dripped like honey through the autumn foliage. The clearing appeared in front of her, quite unexpectedly, after a few minutes. She leaned her bicycle against a tree and pushed on through tall grasses and ferns. Her heart was hammering wildly, and as she climbed the steps, she felt her arms and legs trembling. The trapdoor was heavy. She found the loose plank in the wall, pushed the tightly wrapped packet inside, and replaced the plank. On the way back to the Kalder estate, she kept looking around, as if she expected to be followed. It was not until she had passed the farmhouse that her heartbeat calmed down.

Her father recovered, but when he opened his practice again, only a few patients continued to come. People did not want to be seen with him, and sometimes there was a note in his mailbox: could he perhaps come by that evening—the newborn had a bad cough, the son had had a fall, or the old mother couldn't keep anything down. So it came about that what Margarete Pohl had claimed in the preceding months actually became true. Her husband was out half the night. He was making house calls.

Chapter 14

April 22, 1998

When Rita Albers dialed the Spanish telephone number, it was a Luisa Alfonsi who answered, and there was a short pause before a self-confident voice announced itself as "Mende."

Rita introduced herself, and was hesitating before making her request, when the woman firmly interrupted.

"I know who you are. Get to the point."

Rita was thrown off balance, but she tried not to show how rattled she was. How did Mende know who she was?

"It's about your marriage to Wilhelm Peters," she said quickly.

The woman at the other end of the line reacted immediately. "And?"

"Well, I'd very much like to interview you."

"I don't give interviews."

Rita swallowed hard. She had assumed she would have the element of surprise on her side.

"But you don't deny that you were married to Wilhelm Peters, and that you were suspected of his murder when he disappeared?"

"If you think you've dug up a good story here, you're mistaken. Keep your nose out of it," Mende replied bluntly.

Rita gasped. Who did this woman think she was?

"I'm a journalist, and I'm working on a story, and if you don't wish to comment, I'll publish the results of my research without your statement."

Again the answer came swiftly, and with a level of self-confidence that made Rita nervous.

"You're a naive little thing, you know. I strongly advise you to check your so-called facts very carefully. Other journalists before you have ruined their careers with libels. You can be sure I'll sue you and win. I'll be glad to give you that in writing."

And with that the line went dead.

Rita slammed the receiver down, ran into the garden, and stamped her way across the orchard, snorting with fury. The woman was bluffing. There was no other explanation. She was a successful business-woman, and of course she had had a lot of practice, but she, Rita, was not going to allow herself to be browbeaten. On the other hand, she had often had dealings with canny people who had threatened and abused her, but that had been different. Mende had not hesitated for a second: not the slightest hint of uncertainty. And how had she known who she was?

Once she had regained her composure and headed back toward the terrace, she heard the telephone ringing inside the house.

It was Robert Lubisch. "Frau Albers, the conference is over, and I'm about to leave. I must talk to you."

Rita rolled her eyes and thought for a moment. "All right," she began. "Come and see me. I have some new information that might interest you."

Robert Lubisch had been distracted all day, and he found himself almost unable to follow the presentations. He kept going back to Rita Albers, and the question of what else she would uncover, or what else might happen. This word *happen* felt threatening, and the more he thought about it, the more the word stretched out and howled in his head, rising and falling, like a siren.

He had slept fitfully the previous night, tormented by bad dreams. He dreamed that he was in his parents' house, walking from room to room. He was looking for something, but he didn't know what. Nevertheless, there was this inner certainty that he was on the right path to identify it. His mother was sitting in the kitchen, her head in her bony hands, the bluish veins visible under her parchment skin. She was wearing a black knitted shawl, and when she lowered her hands, her face was astonishingly young. She said, "That's his life's work." She appeared not to see him. She stood up, turned her back on him, and went over to the kitchen door. Her shawl unraveled from top to bottom as she stepped away from him. She kept on walking, without ever reaching the door. Bit by bit, his mother's naked back was exposed, and he knew it was his fault, that he was standing on the yarn, incapable of lifting his foot.

This had made him wake up with a start, the first time, and drink a glass of water. When he went back to sleep, he was walking about in the house again. Once more he was searching, but this time without confidence; instead, he was fearful, and driven by an inexplicable haste. He ran up the broad, curving staircase, two steps at a time, and was again the boy he had once been. He opened every door, and realized he was looking for his father. He found him in the study, sitting in his armchair. It was disproportionately large, and his father sat in it, small, with dangling feet. He had the cigar box in his lap and he said, almost inaudibly, "Come, I'll show it to you."

Eventually he had sat up in bed, bathed in sweat. He had gotten up at four o'clock, afraid of further dreams.

Later, as he listened to a colleague's presentation in the conference room, he remembered an incident during his student days. He had been at home during vacation and had gone to a concert with his parents. His father, who seldom drank, had had some red wine at dinner. During the interval, he drank some sparkling wine, said hello to a large number of people, and introduced his son to them. "This is my son," he said, "the future head of the Lubisch Corporation." Robert did not rise to this, preferring not to argue with his father in public. As they were returning to their seats, his mother took him aside and whispered, "Let him have that. He's so proud of his life's work. Of you and his life's work."

But all he heard was that his father did not respect his decision to become a doctor. Once they were home, they got into one of those arguments that built up over the years, making them grow farther and farther apart.

The old man had clung to his expectations with incredible tenacity, as a consequence ignoring, even denying, anything that did not fit in with his image of the world. What if he had done the same thing with his own history?

Robert felt a flush of heat rising, heard his blood rushing in time with his heartbeat in his inner ear.

What else would this journalist find out?

His colleague's presentation was over, there was noise all around, chairs being pushed back. He sat where he was.

His father was dead. The woman in the photo had not been his father's lover, and he had not wanted to know any more. He would not allow this journalist woman to drag his father's life out into the open.

Chapter 15

April 22, 1998

To begin with, her short telephone conversation with Rita Albers had provoked Therese Mende to anger, but then this had turned into a kind of impassivity. It had become a vacuum in which her thoughts moved slowly and viscously. She picked up the silver-framed picture of her daughter from the sideboard. Beside it stood the picture, still bearing a black ribbon, of her husband, Tillmann. He would have known how to talk to Isabel. He would have found the right words. But she herself? How was she supposed to tell her grown-up daughter the thing she had kept secret all these years? Isabel was strong, of that there was no doubt. She would know how to handle it. But how would she behave toward her mother in the future? Could Therese bear it if her daughter turned against her, if she wouldn't forgive the lies about her past?

Rita Albers, filled with blind journalistic zeal, was in the process of destroying her life.

She put the picture down. That woman would try to sell her story to the highest bidder. It was about money. Of course, it was always about money.

The realization was liberating, and it set her in motion. She spent more than an hour on the phone with her lawyer. Then she sat down on the terrace, beneath the eaves, and felt the tension dropping away. It would be a matter of the right price.

But for herself there was no escape. The time that had been kept secret was relentlessly demanding its rightful place, now that the first images had revealed themselves. Whenever she found herself at rest, it was like an undertow from which she could not pull free.

Christmas 1939

For the first half of December, Kranenburg was like a sketch in soft charcoal. Snow lay heaped on the roofs. The fields and meadows were laid out like huge bleached sheets on wash day. Avenues of poplars stood like smudged lines in the colorless silence. Toward the lake, hungry crows cawed from bare trees.

A damp, heavy chill forced people to hurry through the streets with their heads bowed.

Therese joined the League of German Girls, and her mother joined the National Socialist Women's League. It was a family decision, whereby they hoped to escape general attention. And peace did in fact return to the Pohl household. A sensitive, concentrated peace, a kind of still watchfulness.

During the last few weeks, she had cycled to the lookout three times to drop off or pick up papers.

From time to time she met up with Wilhelm, who would now be seen publicly with her in places where she "belonged." They went for walks, or went to the little café by the church. His pale blue eyes would light up in honest joy when he looked at her. Sometimes he would outline his plans. Across the table in the café he whispered that he wanted a big family; during a walk he told her he dreamed of leaving Kranenburg, moving to a big city, and taking on really big assignments. Then he would wait, and it seemed to Therese that he was hoping for a sign. A signal that would give him the courage to talk about his attraction again.

Shortly before Christmas, the beautiful whiteness everywhere disappeared, and the winter became unusually mild. When Alwine came home at the beginning of the Christmas holidays, it was raining. A narrow strip of slush at the edge of the street was the only reminder that it was winter.

Alwine, filled with excitement, talked about her boarding school and life in Düsseldorf. She modeled nail varnish and lipstick, wore elegant shoes with high heels, and showed off a tight blue suit like the ones the women in fashion magazines wore. She told stories about everyday life at school, with its roll call in front of the flag and its marching drill, and the punishment she could expect if she was caught with lipstick or pumps. Then she laughed her infectious laugh, and Therese realized how she had missed Alwine. She could listen to her for hours. The red plaits had disappeared; now she wore her hair loose, shoulder length. Over her forehead was a perfect quiff, held in place with little hair combs. She told them how she and her schoolmates would sneak into a pub where musicians played on weekends, and demonstrated swing dancing and the fox-trot. And again and again she asked after Wilhelm. How was he, had Therese seen him, and had he talked about her, Alwine?

That evening, as Therese rode along the narrow tracks between the water meadows and the fields, she was downcast. She had not had the courage to tell Alwine about Wilhelm's declaration. Nor had she mentioned her father's arrest.

Years later, Therese Mende would tell her second husband about this evening and say she felt guilty. Not because Wilhelm loved her and not Alwine, but because she did not love Wilhelm. Because she was taking something away from Alwine, only to reject it.

And then, the day before Christmas Eve, Jacob came home on leave, without Leonard.

She was waiting on the platform, alongside Hanna, Alwine, and Wilhelm, as Leonard's father came out of the little station building and approached them along the platform. Kramer, the lawyer, was a short, plump man with earnest features and a stiffness that had made Therese shy when she was a child.

On this day he seemed relaxed. He was even smiling.

When the train came in and only Jacob stepped out, she saw him turn pale. For a moment it seemed that only the formal black wool coat, gray hat, and glistening leather shoes were standing on the platform—a motionless exhibit draped over a coat hanger.

Jacob had changed. The remnants of his youthfulness had disappeared. He seemed even taller in his uniform, and one could see the effect of physical work in fresh air.

"Leonard didn't get leave," he said, his eyes wandering evasively across the tracks.

From somewhere between the gray hat and the black coat, Therese heard Kramer's voice.

"Why not?"

Jacob shook his head and said, with a bitterness that Therese had never heard in him before, "Because the fieldmaster felt like it."

The hat and coat turned, and the leather shoes went back into the station. Jacob ran after him and grabbed him by the sleeve. He joined Kramer in the car, and they drove off.

The platform emptied. Some strolled off arm in arm, laughing and gesticulating, others in a hurry, hats pulled down over their faces. The train released its brakes with a hiss. The wheels hammered out their laborious, then gradually quickening, rhythm, and it echoed beneath the tin roof of the platform. To Therese, it was overwhelming. Jacob's suitcase lay a few steps away from her. Left behind!

Therese waited. Slowly she paced along the edge of the platform, peering in the direction from which the train had arrived and willing it to arrive again.

Hanna stared at the Kramers' car as it left, Jacob sitting inside it. Jacob, who had barely said hello to her.

Wilhelm was the first to collect himself. He picked up Jacob's suitcase. They left the station in silence.

A squalling wind was driving rain across the forecourt. Until Jacob arrived, she had felt Christmassy anticipation, despite the weather. She had thought she would have all her friends around her again after a long time.

That evening, around seven, she was having supper by candlelight with her parents, behind blacked-out windows, when someone hammered on the door. This happened frequently, but ever since her father's arrest, there was always an anxious pause in the Pohl household before one of them warily opened the curtain a crack and peered out.

It was Jacob. He had not gone home yet; he had spent the last few hours at the Kramers'.

Margarete Pohl pressed him down onto the kitchen bench and laid another plate. Jacob looked at Siegmund Pohl and said, "I'm sorry." He leaned back and rubbed his face with his hands. "About your arrest, I mean. I heard about it from Kramer just now."

Therese was amazed. Apart from Wilhelm, nobody in the town had mentioned it until now.

And then Jacob told them about Leonard.

There were twenty-five of them when they arrived at the camp. They had gotten to know some of their comrades on the train. Many, like Jacob and Leonard, had applied for officer training.

Leonard attracted Fieldmaster Köbe's attention on the very first day. Köbe was standing in the quartermaster's stores, feet apart, beside the men issuing work clothes and uniforms. Every new arrival had to unpack his suitcase on the counter in front of him. Like many others, Leonard had some books in his, among them volumes of poetry by Mörike, Goethe, and Rilke. Köbe grinned at him. "Well, look at this. We're getting a real intellectual in our humble huts. Poetry!" He leaned over and said, "You'll soon learn this isn't a holiday camp. We're going to make a man of you." He took the volumes of poetry and placed them on a shelf. "When your time here is up, you can have them back. If you still want them by then."

They spent the first few days in constant exercises. A spade stood in for their weapon. Fieldmaster Köbe's favorite was making them crawl across the concrete parade ground, with its scattering of frozen puddles, in the early hours of the morning. At night he would whistle them out of bed; they had to muster in the yard in full work clothes. If their uniform was not absolutely perfect, he would make them stand at attention for hours, crawl under barbed wire on the practice field, or climb the wall on the obstacle course over and over again. Almost every day, it was Leonard who was singled out by Fieldmaster Köbe or Commander Grosse. "Civilian asshole," they called him, or "pointless intellectual." At first, Jacob, and some of their other comrades too, intervened. Then they were made to undergo "special training" themselves, along with Leonard. When they did not give up but kept protesting, Köbe changed tack. In return for every remark from the others, Leonard received further "physical strengthening exercises."

They spent the day clearing a path through an area of forest, digging up tree stumps and root systems. When they returned to camp, exhausted, drill began. His voice dripping with sarcasm, Köbe called this "preparing the prospective gentleman officers for their future duties." Leonard had already collapsed twice and been taken to the sick bay.

Jacob stared hollowly at the table, apparently drawing these images from the worn surface of the wood. Occasionally he looked around in distress, as if he himself could not believe what he was telling them. As if he were only now becoming aware of its monstrousness.

Then he wept like a child. "I don't understand. We're good National Socialists after all, faithfully supporting the Führer."

Therese Mende would remember that evening again at the end of the 1970s. At the time, she was living in London, and an archaeologist friend was visiting. He told them he had once spent two days trapped underground after an accident during an excavation. He said, "The powers of human beings are beyond our belief. We can withstand the most incredible things, when there's no way out. It's not until we talk about them later, when we try to express them in words, that we cry. Because it's not true until then."

At that moment, in her mind's eye, she had seen Jacob on the kitchen bench again. He was groping for words, looking up in disbelief at each phrase he found, as if he were listening to someone else's story.

On the day after Christmas, Therese went to the Kalders'. The atmosphere was oppressive. Alwine was the only one attempting to spread a bit of cheer. She had been given a fur stole, and she pulled Therese into her room. Once inside, she twirled in front of the mirror, the stole pulled high around her throat or thrown loosely over her shoulders.

Therese distractedly congratulated her on her gift. For the first time, she found Alwine's joie de vivre selfish and shallow.

"How can you make such a fuss over that stupid bit of fur?" she snapped. "Don't you care about Leonard?"

Alwine burst into tears. The stole fell to the ground, unheeded, and she covered her face with her hands. She burst out, almost unintelligibly, "I can't help it, Therese. Don't you understand? I can't help it!"

Feeling ashamed, she sat down on the bed beside Alwine.

Years later, Therese told her second husband how she realized for the first time that afternoon that Alwine's lightheartedness was a kind of escape. "Alwine," she said, "was a person on the run. Staying on the surface was the only way she could survive."

As Therese was leaving, she spoke briefly to Jacob at the door. "My father will try to get Leonard out of there," he said in a monotone. He shrugged helplessly. Then he forced out a short, joyless smile. "I'm sure he'll succeed."

Therese did not ask after Hanna. Hanna had receded into the background for all of them, Leonard's fate having become more important. It was not until several days later, when Jacob had already left, that Therese found out that he had visited Hanna again and that they had quarreled. "Leonard, Leonard, Leonard," Hanna had berated him in a rage. "So go back to your Leonard!"

Chapter 16

April 23, 1998

Two workmen from Schoofs, the landscape gardeners, rang Rita Alberss doorbell. Her car was parked in the carport, and when there was no movement inside the house, they tried again. Then they went into the garden. They had orders to measure for a new well between the terrace and the vegetable garden, and to check the soil composition. While they were examining the land, one of them looked over at the terrace door, which stood ajar. They went up the steps, calling out, "Hello! Hello, Frau Albers. Are you there?"

They saw it before they even reached the door. Papers and files lay on the floor in a chaotic mess. A puddle of water and the large, curved shards of a glass vase glittered among them. Red and yellow tulips, their petals already limp and dying, added a few splashes of color to the surreal still life.

"Shit." The younger of the two shoved his hands into the pockets of his overalls while the older man called out "Frau Albers" again, this time more emphatically, and it was as if he were sounding a warning. They hesitated momentarily, then quickly crossed the room. They found Rita Albers in the kitchen. She was sitting in one of the beige chairs, her head resting on the table, like someone who has slumped forward drunk or dead tired. Her hair was red and sticky, and there were red lines with droplet-shaped ends drying on the chair, like spilt oil paint.

They stood stock-still for several seconds before the older man ran back into the devastated living room for the telephone on the desk.

Karl van den Boom, of the Kranenburg police station, was the first on the scene, and he informed his Homicide colleagues in Kalkar. "Not nice," he said into the radio of his patrol car. "Not nice at all. You'd better have a look for yourselves." He listened patiently and, after a while, said calmly, "Of course she's dead, my dear colleague. Do you think I'm calling you because she's dancing naked in the garden?"

He crossed the terrace and went back into the house. From the door, he studied the damage.

He took the two gardeners out to the front of the house. Leaning against his patrol car, he took their statements. What had they touched, he wanted to know. "Just the phone," the older one said. "Oh, and one or two pieces of paper while I was looking for it."

"And the sink, for me," said the other one. "I held on to it because . . . I just couldn't believe what I was seeing." Van den Boom nodded, uttering sympathetic uh-huhs from time to time and making notes while waiting for his colleagues from Serious Crime. He had hoped Manfred Steiner would be with them, but when they arrived, it was six-foot-six Brand, to whom he had spoken on the telephone, who climbed out of the car. Karl van den Boom watched them cordon off a large area around the crime scene, slip on latex gloves, and pull on white overalls; when flashbulbs started going off inside the house, he reflected that Rita Albers was now a big story in her own right and that she was witnessing her last photo session. He was reminded of how much in a hurry she had been the day before, and it occurred to him that when people hurried, they reached their end that much more quickly.

Two hours later, as Rita Albers was being taken away in a plastic box, he got into his car and drove to Kleve. The Peters file lay on the passenger seat; it ought to be in its rightful place in the police archives when he told his colleagues the following morning that Rita Albers had been interested in this old case.

Chapter 17

April 23, 1998

Therese Mende was in her study, going through her mail, when the telephone rang and Hanna announced herself. "The Albers woman is dead." She fell silent. The study was on the first floor, and Therese could look down onto her neighbor's property, at the swimming pool with its kitsch cherubs dispensing water from amphorae at the four corners.

"How?" she asked after several seconds, leaning heavily against the windowsill.

"People are saying she was beaten to death." She could hear Hanna breathing heavily. "Paul should never have rented out the cottage. Father's turning in his grave."

Therese's thoughts came thick and fast. She did not hear the last few phrases. "Hanna, do you know whether that woman was working on the story alone?" Hanna did not hesitate for long. "I think so, yes. Yes, I'm certain of it. She was that kind."

Therese felt the tension of the last few days leave her. "Keep me up to date," she said as she brought the conversation to a close. A light breeze ruffled the pale pink bougainvillea that grew over the walls of her property. She thought she heard a faint rustling sound.

There had been a wind back then too, but it had been icy.

February 1940

SS officers were now housed in the town hall, the Brown House, and even in the pastor's home. More soldiers kept arriving, and they were billeted in private homes. Her father was certain they were preparing for the invasion of Holland.

On the afternoon she saw Leonard again, a blustery wind was driving dense clouds across the sky. The smell of damp cold lay in the air, a moisture that clung tightly to streets, houses, and clothes.

At first she did not recognize him. He came toward her, the collar of his dark blue wool coat raised and a scarf wrapped protectively around his mouth and nose. They had been about to pass each other, when he stopped.

"Therese?" She recognized his voice immediately. He removed the scarf from his face. The high cheekbones had always made him look somewhat gaunt, but now, with his high forehead, they dominated his face. His eyes, his mouth, his chin—everything seemed to retreat behind his prominent bones.

She dropped her purse and, giving in to her first impulse, folded him in her arms out in the street.

Later, when she remembered this moment, she could still feel his emaciated body. Although Leonard was taller than she was, she had felt as if she were holding a delicate little bird.

"I've been discharged," he said tonelessly. "I won't be doing officer training. I'm not fit for service." He emphasized the word *fit* with a hostility that was directed against himself, that branded him a failure.

A few days before, she had received a letter from Jacob. About events in the camp, he wrote:

> When I got back here after my Christmas leave, some of our comrades had made sure Leonard was transferred to the sick bay. They had come in at noon one day and found him lying in his cot with a high fever.
>
> He had a serious inflammation of the lungs. As I was packing his things, I found some of his clothes completely soaked. Holger Becker, who had not been allowed Christmas leave either, told me Köbe had made Leonard go do exercises almost as soon as we had gone. He decided Leo wasn't trying his hardest, so he emptied a bucket of water over him in the freezing cold; then he had to go on exercising in his wet clothes. So New Year's Eve wasn't a particularly happy celebration here, but not long after, on January 5, there was an unannounced health check for all officer candidates. Leonard was discharged immediately and sent to a hospital in Münster as a civilian. The doctor didn't pay much attention to the rest of us at all. We had the impression he had come with Leonard's transfer papers already filled out. So Father kept his promise.

She met up with Leonard from time to time, and they went on long walks. He never talked about his time in the Labor Service, and yet his experiences lay between the lines of everything he said, everything he did. The sadness that had enveloped him since he got back never went away. Not that they did not laugh and joke with each other, but he never regained the confident self-belief with which he had climbed into the train alongside Jacob.

Köbe, she realized years later, had ruined Leonard's conception of humanity. For anyone else, this would have meant approaching the world with mistrust for ever after. But Leonard could not do that. Leonard turned away. And it was therefore unbearably lonely to walk beside him.

Therese had not gone back to the lookout for months. The Pohls' house was continually watched, and in May her father's prediction was fulfilled. Holland capitulated after only five days. Germany was in an ecstasy of victory. It was a contagious frenzy from which she could scarcely escape. The newsreels showed German soldiers in the occupied territories. Denmark, Norway, Holland, and Belgium had capitulated, and German troops were in Paris. The screen showed beaming soldiers in conquerors' poses, welcomed by jubilant crowds in every nation.

Leonard stayed home all summer, convalescing. After that, in accordance with his parents' wishes, he was to study law in Cologne. Therese visited him often, and would find him reading in the Kramers' garden as soon as the weather permitted. He would often get up early in the morning and hike in the Klever Reichswald for hours, alone. Occasionally, when he was lost in a book or exhausted after his walking, she felt as if she saw the Leonard of old again. She could sense the serene joy he seemed to feel when he dived into the world of his books, when a poem moved him, or when he had spent a day in the midst of nature, far from human beings.

One Sunday in June, she walked over to the Kalders' with Wilhelm and Leonard. She and Alwine had passed their school-leaving exams. They wanted to spend the afternoon in the company of old friends, and Alwine had invited them over for coffee and cake.

They sat on benches in the yard, separated by the rectangle of the rough wooden table with its tablecloth. Therese was pouring coffee and Alwine was bringing out some cake, when Hanna joined them. They welcomed her happily.

They chatted about this and that, and Leonard told them what Jacob, who had begun his officer training, had written in his most recent letter. Hanna asked, almost casually, "How often do you write to each other?" He answered immediately, "Every week." Hanna flinched, as if struck by a whip.

For three gossamer-thin seconds, there was silence—a membrane of time that could not endure.

Then Wilhelm leapt to his feet and shouted at Leonard, asking whether he didn't notice what he had been doing for weeks. "You're coming between Jacob and Hanna and between me and Therese." At this his voice cracked and took on an almost tearful tone.

The remaining images of that afternoon were without color, the friends' faces waxen. Even the red blooms of the rambling rose against the wall of the house were pale and translucent.

Leonard, staring at Wilhelm in disbelief. Hanna, jumping to her feet and running away. And Alwine, eyes flicking incredulously from Wilhelm to Therese and back, turning away as if in slow motion and disappearing into the house.

Later, Therese would often wonder whether everything began with that afternoon, or whether there was a kind of inevitability about it, whether they had been heading that way for years, perhaps since they were children setting off for school together for the first time.

On that Sunday in June, Therese went back to Kranenburg with Wilhelm and told him she did not love him. He walked alongside her in silence, his hands in his trouser pockets, and she was relieved at how calmly he took it.

Three weeks later, Jacob came back on a visit, and one evening he told Hanna—undoubtedly more skillfully and with more tact than she had used with Wilhelm—the same thing. During that summer, the devastating power of rejected love took form.

Chapter 18

April 23, 1998

By the time Robert Lubisch came on duty at the hospital at eight o'clock, his stay in Kranenburg, his conversations with Rita Albers, and his anxious fears seemed like some distant nightmare.

She had greeted him curtly on the Wednesday afternoon, telling him at the door that she was going to write the story anyway and that no one was going to stop her. Then she had gone into the kitchen, and since she had left the door open, he had taken it as an invitation. He asked what she might get for such a story, and she burst out laughing. "Yesterday," she said, "it would still have been a local-interest story, but today it looks quite different. The price has shot through the roof in the course of a day."

He flinched, but he did not allow himself to be sidetracked. He was determined not to leave without a satisfactory result.

She offered him tea, and they sat down at the kitchen table again. Her movements were agitated, and she fumed that she was not to be bought off, and why did the whole world suddenly believe she was? He reflected that he had found her attractive two days ago, and that it was because of the way she moved that this was no longer true. When at last she sat down, she said, "Your father's story doesn't interest me, and if it's important to you, I can promise it won't appear in my article. Your father took the papers from Peters while he was still alive—we'll never know whether knowingly or unknowingly—and it doesn't matter anymore. I'm interested in Wilhelm and Therese Peters." She went on to say she had found Therese Peters. That she had gotten married in Frankfurt in 1956, using her maiden name, and that Wilhelm's disappearance had never been explained. But Robert Lubisch was only half listening; he was busy feeling relieved and wanted nothing more to do with all that.

As he drove back to Hamburg, he listened to a Ravel piece for oboe, bassoon, and piano, and let his thoughts wander, as he liked to do when the motorway was not crowded. He was relieved, not only because Rita Albers would not be writing about his father, but also because the legend of the quick-witted young hero who had made his way through the confusion of war, unerring and untarnished, had been recalibrated. A crack had appeared in the facade of the larger-than-life Friedhelm Lubisch. Uninteresting for Rita Albers, but important for him, his son.

It was past midnight by the time he got home. Maren, who worked as a freelance interpreter, was in Brussels for a week, and he went straight up to bed.

Having finished his rounds in the children's ward around midday, he was heading for the canteen when a nurse came running after him. "Dr. Lubisch," she called out. "Wait. The police are in your office. They want to talk to you."

Robert Lubisch raised his eyebrows and turned back. He had regular dealings with the police in cases of child abuse, but he did not have any such cases on the ward at present.

A man and a rather young woman were standing in his office. He shook hands with them both, then looked at them expectantly. The man, who had introduced himself as Söters, asked, "Dr. Lubisch, do you know a Rita Albers?"

Robert heard the name as if with a delay. In this room it sounded strange, out of place.

"Yes," he said. Then, innocently, "A journalist in Kranenburg." He paused for a moment and added, "Why do you ask?"

Söters pursed his moist, fleshy lips and replied with a question of his own: "When did you see her last?"

Lubisch became uneasy. He did not know whether it was due to the police officer's mouth, which he found repellent, or his question. "Yesterday evening," he said, truthfully, "but what's this about?"

The female officer—he had not caught her name—took over. "What was the nature of your relationship with her?"

"Relationship?" Robert shook his head. Then, for the first time, he realized she had used the past tense. "What do you mean, *was*?"

"Answer the question," said the moist mouth, and Robert Lubisch sensed an inexplicable menace.

"I first met Frau Albers three days ago, and I last saw her yesterday evening."

"When?" Again the thick, wet lips, like a dog snatching at something.

He was suddenly gripped by anger. "All right, that's enough now. If you don't tell me what's going on, I'll ask you to get out of my office. I won't be treated like this."

The officers exchanged a glance. "Frau Albers is dead," the woman said. "She was murdered yesterday evening."

Lubisch took a step back and leaned against the windowsill. "But that's impossible," he whispered.

The officers looked at him expectantly.

"Look, I left Frau Albers at about eight o'clock, and she was alive."

He sat down at his desk and invited the two officers to sit down too. He gave a truthful account, mentioned the photograph and his interest in it. He did not mention the identity papers. After all, Rita Albers herself had said they were not important.

They asked whether he had noticed anything the previous evening, but he could remember only that her movements lacked fluidity. "She told me she had found Therese Peters," he recalled. The woman took a notebook from her jacket, wrote something down, and asked, "Where would we find this Frau Peters?" He shrugged. "She didn't say." The woman looked at him suspiciously and, as if closing the conversation, made a note. "We'll pass that on to our colleagues in the lower Rhine," she said, and Lubisch, somewhat absently, took this as a request for his permission. "Yes. Yes, do that," he said, nodding, but he was already thinking about something else. "Tell me, how did you find out about me?"

The man smiled, and indicated with a nod to his female colleague that she could answer. Lubisch wondered whether she liked Söters's mouth, red and naked as it was, rather as if he had licked it raw.

"The dead woman," she said, "had your business card in her trouser pocket."

Robert nodded. "I gave it to her the first time we met."

Söters stood up. "Keep yourself available," he growled at Robert Lubisch, then signaled to the woman that she should follow him. At the door, she turned to him again. "Did you give Frau Albers the photo? The original, I mean. Or have you still got it?"

He stood up, went to the closet, and took the photo of Therese Peters out of the breast pocket of his jacket.

"Can we keep this?"

Robert Lubisch nodded; he was almost glad to give it away. Once they had gone, he remained in his seat for a while. What had he gotten himself into? Could it be that Rita Albers had had to die because she had been looking for Therese Peters? But that was crazy.

He stood up and went down to the canteen. Rita Albers, with her demanding style, must have made many enemies. It occurred to him that the police would find not only the copy of the photo in her house but also the scanned documents on her computer.

In the cafeteria, he placed a cup under the coffee machine and pressed "Cappuccino." He would say it had not seemed important to him.

He helped himself to a cheese sandwich and sat down alone at a table. He felt uneasy. "Keep yourself available," that Söters had said. Was he suspected of murder? And what if Rita Albers really had had to die because he . . .

Chapter 19

April 23, 1998

Therese Mende stood on the terrace and watched the cirrus clouds gathering in the west, piling up against one another and heading for the island. The wind had freshened; the beginner surfers were being brought back to shore in a boat, while the advanced ones were looking optimistically up at the sky and rigging smaller sails.

1940/41

Wilhelm was on a six-month course in Stuttgart, and Therese was doing her labor service with the cattle on the Kruse farm. The Kruses were simple, kindly people. They often gave her a jug of milk in the evening, or a bag of potatoes or vegetables.

Alwine was studying history in Cologne. After that afternoon, Therese had written her a letter and tried to explain that she felt nothing for Wilhelm, but Alwine did not react. A week later she left.

Leonard was to take up a university place in Cologne too, but he could not start until the summer semester. He spent the winter at home, helping his father out in his chambers in Kleve.

SS Captain Hollmann kept an eye on Siegmund Pohl. At times he had the medical practice watched so visibly that the few patients who had remained loyal to him were forced to notice, and they would only rarely dare to come to his door. In September, Siegmund Pohl stopped taking down the "Practice Closed" sign that normally hung in the window on Sundays.

He sat in the kitchen for hours, staring ahead. When he went out, to the pub or, on Saturdays, to the market, people would avoid him, not wanting to be seen with someone like him. He lived like a stranger among former patients and friends.

In late October, Therese was sitting in the garden with her father. They were peeling apples, which her mother was preserving in the kitchen. It was one of those mild autumn days that shimmer in the memory. Days on which the trees stand taller. Margarete Pohl came into the garden with the letter and handed it wordlessly to her husband. Under "Subject" it said: "Termination of leasehold." It went on:

> Since this is a matter of housing space for the community, which is urgently required for other purposes, and your leasehold agreement specifies the operation of a medical practice, we must demand that you leave the house by the end of the year.

Hollmann had signed it.

"Let's leave," her father said, and she thought she heard relief and optimism in that "leave." But her mother wanted to stay. She continued going to church every day, in the firm belief that things would change soon. "God will not put up with this much longer," she said with deep conviction, wagging her finger at the invisible enemy.

They spent a month searching for a home, without success. Some people looked down with embarrassment and shrugged regretfully; the faces of others showed satisfaction. They crossed their arms confidently over their chests as they spat out their "no." One Monday in early December—it was becoming clear that they would not find a home in Kranenburg—there was a knock on the door, and Hanna's father, Gustav Höver, stood on the threshold. The old man, who must have been approaching sixty, was tall and big-boned, and had the typical round Höver face, with its permanently flushed cheeks. He did not accept the seat her father offered but remained standing in the middle of the kitchen, wringing his peaked cap in his plate-sized hands. He reached into his coat pocket, pulled out a key, and laid it on the kitchen table.

"It belongs to the cottage. If you want, Doctor, you can live there." Then he left. Her father leapt to his feet and ran after him, but Höver turned and raised his hands defensively. "I'm ashamed," he said, his head down. "I'm ashamed of what's happening here."

They moved a week later. Hollmann came to inspect the vacated house in person. He strode about among the boxes and furniture, and it was soon obvious that he was to be the new tenant.

They transported the first few loads on a handcart, but there was too much furniture and it was too big. They could neither carry it nor install it in the cottage. Hollmann smiled condescendingly and offered to take the furniture off their hands. "I'll give you a good price," he said. "You can't take it away anyway."

By about midday—they could barely move the heavy oak dresser in the living room, let alone transport it on a handcart—her father was ready to negotiate. Hollmann made an all-encompassing gesture and named a ridiculous price. Her mother wept with rage, and for a second time threatened God's punishment. Then a horse and cart stopped in front of the house, and Gustav Höver came in. Hollmann roared at Höver to make himself scarce, but the old man stood right in front of him and said, "We're loading the furniture onto the cart." He said it quite neutrally, in a completely matter-of-fact way. They made three trips, storing the biggest and heaviest pieces in Höver's barn.

Later, Therese Mende enjoyed remembering that scene. At the time, she had thought Höver had some kind of hold on Hollmann. It was not until years after the war that she understood that it was Höver's determination, his way of standing there and holding one's gaze: Hollmann was not used to it and did not know how to react.

Christmas in their new home was modest. Wrapped up in coats and scarves, they trudged through driving snow toward the blacked-out settlement of Kranenburg, close to two miles distant, for Midnight Mass. The church was packed, its windows covered with light-blocking material. After Mass, they stood in the square in front of the church as they did every year, shaking hands and wishing one another a happy Christmas. They were all there: Jacob and Alwine, Hanna, Leonard, and Wilhelm. But they did not stand together, as in previous years. She chatted briefly with Jacob and Leonard. Jacob's training had been cut short, and after his home leave, he was to go to the front. She saw the tears in Leonard's eyes. Alwine and Wilhelm stood next to each other. Hanna did not shake hands with any of the friends; she did not wish anyone a happy Christmas. When Jacob approached her, she left the square. They set off for home with the Hövers. Therese and Hanna had little Paul Höver between them; her parents walked a few paces behind them with old Höver. The wind had let up a little, and the snowflakes were falling gently and almost vertically. A clear, weightless silence lay over the fields and meadows, and the only sound was the muffled rhythm of their steps, the soft crunching of snow underfoot.

"The way Leo looks at Jacob, that's not normal," Hanna said, her voice harsh. She walked on, calm and regular, as if she had been talking to herself.

"What do you mean?" asked Therese, but Hanna shook her head angrily and said nothing.

Four weeks later, she would remember her words. Four weeks later, she would learn for the first time what unimaginable love was capable of. Unimaginable!

Therese Mende was freezing. The west wind was piling up the clouds and driving them toward the bay. Spray leapt high over the rocks, and the droplets of water celebrated their brief freedom with a dance before falling back into the green darkness of the sea. Surfers in wet suits stood belly-deep in the water, holding boards and sails overhead and trying to get past the breakers.

Chapter 20

April 23, 1998

Sergeant Karl van den Boom sat at his desk. He had brought back the missing-persons file on Peters and had spoken to Frau Jäckel from the registration office. Now he was writing down what he, or rather Rita Albers, had found out. He studied his notes, muttering angrily to himself, then called Homicide. He got Brand.

"Something I missed this morning: Albers was here yesterday, interested in an old missing-persons case," he said evenly. For half a minute he listened, eyes closed, then said, "Have you finished? . . . Good. Would you like to know the case she was interested in?" He was silent again for several seconds, during which he drew some geometrical shapes on his blotter.

"It was Peters. The Peters case, from the 1950s. The files are in Kleve. I told her so, and that's where I sent her."

Then, casually, he asked, "How far have you got? I mean, do you have anything yet?"

"Hmm . . . Hmm . . . Yes. So yes . . . Bye."

He hung up and wrote on a sheet of notepaper:

R. Albers found T. Peters?
Laptop stolen.
Dr. Robert Lubisch, Hamburg.

At six o'clock Van den Boom closed the little police station and drove to the Höver farm. Bronco, the Hövers' sheepdog, was off his leash and leapt toward him happily as he got out of his car. He walked around the back, crossed the covered yard, knocked on the metal door that led to the living quarters, and walked in. Bronco stayed close and tried to slip into the kitchen. "Leave the dog outside," said Hanna, without looking up. She was sitting at the kitchen table with Paul, eating supper. The aroma of freshly baked bread and smoked ham mingled with the omnipresent bitter smell of horses. Bronco looked at Karl, disappointed, as he pushed him back with his foot. Van den Boom was still in uniform, and Hanna looked him up and down suspiciously.

He looked down at himself and shook his head. "No, no. I'm not here on duty . . . Just haven't gotten around to . . ."

Paul busied himself with his meal. "What is it then?" he asked casually.

Karl pulled back one of the old wooden chairs and sat down. "*Guten Appetit*, first of all. Smells good in this house."

Hanna stood up, laid a plate and glass before him, and then a knife. She fetched a bottle of beer from the refrigerator. "You're not on duty, or are you?"

"No, no." Van den Boom helped himself enthusiastically, and was full of praise for the fresh, warm bread and the home-smoked ham. They talked about the weather, and Paul cursed the wild rabbits that devoured the seedlings in his vegetable garden.

"You know what's happened?" Karl ventured after a longish pause. Paul glanced up. "Your colleagues were already here."

"So, what was she like?" asked Karl, after two more mouthfuls, both thoroughly chewed. "Albers, I mean."

"We had nothing to do with her, really," replied Hanna, taking a sip of beer.

"Sometimes she would come here wanting a bit of advice about the garden. Didn't know how to prune fruit trees, or was having trouble with voles," her brother went on. He busied himself with the ham, cut a few slices, and offered them to Karl.

"Oh, thank you. With pleasure."

There was another pause. Karl had plenty of time.

"Tell me . . . I heard from my colleagues that Albers was interested in Wilhelm and Therese Peters. Do you still remember them? They lived in your cottage, after all."

Hanna nodded, looking him in the eye. "Yes . . . so?"

"Tell me about them." Karl took a sip of his beer and leaned back.

"Ancient history," she said, taking a bite of bread.

Karl looked at Paul, who pushed his plate to one side.

"What do you want to know?"

"Everything."

Paul snorted. "Wilhelm Peters took off, left his wife in the lurch. Beginning of the fifties, that was. A few weeks later, Therese was gone too."

"And . . . did you ever hear from her?"

They both shook their heads.

"Fact is," said Karl, trying to keep the conversation going, "Albers found Frau Peters."

Hanna was still looking at him intently. "So why don't you go to the Peters woman and put your questions to *her*?" She stood up and gathered the plates together, a clear sign that the conversation was at an end, as far as she was concerned.

Karl reached for his beer. "Does the name Lubisch mean anything to you?"

Hanna continued to clear the table. "Should it? Who is it?"

"A doctor from Hamburg. My colleagues tell me he was the one who got Rita Albers asking around about Peters."

Brother and sister exchanged a glance.

"I mean," Karl went on, "nobody asked you about Peters, or did they?"

"Yes." Hanna stood with her back to the table, loading the dishwasher. "Albers asked."

"What did you tell her? You must know that Frau Peters was a murder suspect back then."

Hanna spun round and placed her balled-up fists on her hips. Her pale blue eyes glittered with rage. "Stuff and nonsense! The police back then did everything they could to make out it was murder and pin it on her. But there wasn't even a body."

Karl tried not to show his surprise. He had seldom seen Hanna like this, and he tried to take advantage of her anger. "Hmm. I don't know what happened back then. But now a woman is dead, and I do believe she died because she was asking questions."

Hanna picked up her cardigan from the back of the chair and pulled it on. "I'm going to shut up the stables now," she told her brother, in a tone that sounded like an order to do the same. Then she went out into the covered yard.

Paul stayed where he was, looking at the little blue flowers arranged like a garland on the tablecloth.

"Gerhard was in charge of you people back then," he said. "Maybe you should talk to him. He was friendly with Wilhelm Peters. Shared history, you know." He stood up.

"Wait. What do you mean?"

They went out into the yard. "I don't mean anything, but if you must root about in all that old rubbish, at least start in the right place. Ask Gerhard about the last years of the war."

The evening was turning to dusk, the spring air was mild, and a last, slender strip of reddish-orange light lay in the western sky. As they stood by Karl's car, saying good-bye, they looked over at the small house on the edge of the forest, as if to mark the end of their conversation, and paused. One of the windows was brightly lit.

Chapter 21

April 23, 1998

When she thought back to the year 1941, it was primarily the last days with Leonard that she remembered.

The winter of 1940/41 was one of the coldest ever, and February 14, a Friday, was so cold that Therese had tied a scarf tightly around her mouth and nose. She was cycling home from the Kruse farm. What daylight remained lay in a thin violet band over Holland, and when she dismounted in front of the Kramers' house, the moisture from her breathing had collected in her scarf, freezing it stiff so that it stuck to her cheeks. Frau Kruse had given her a basket of winter apples, and Therese wanted to drop some of them off here. Frau Kramer opened the door. Leonard was in a good mood and invited her in for a cup of tea. Alwine had written to him to say she had found a room for him in Cologne from March 1, and he wanted to take the train there the following day to sign the lease.

"What else does she say?" asked Therese, still hoping that Alwine's grudge against her might have cooled. Leonard laid his hand on her arm and said, "When I'm in Cologne, I'll explain it all to her one more time. She's stubborn—you know that. Give her a little time."

When the doorbell rang, he stood up and called out to his mother, who was busy in the kitchen. "I'll go."

She could hear him say it, even now, in his earnest, yet innocent, way. As he went out, she felt a touch of sadness at the thought that soon Leonard would be gone too. She had seen him strolling through the streets of the big city with Alwine.

The bay now lay beneath a thick layer of cloud. The little sails of the windsurfers danced on the sea, and Therese Mende went into the house because the wind was now unpleasantly chilly. Once in the living room, she felt slightly faint, as she often did recently. She took off her shoes and lay on the sofa.

She remembered the confusion of voices; she heard Leonard's mother running into the hall, shouting, "No!" and, "But why?"

She had gone out into the hall. There were two men in suits standing there. One of them had Leonard by the arm. "Don't make things difficult," the other one said, and then they pulled Leonard toward a car by the side of the road. Frau Kramer grabbed Leo's coat and her own from the wardrobe and ran after them, out into the darkness. "I'm coming too," she cried, but one of the men pushed her back roughly. She stumbled, regained her balance, and held up Leonard's coat. "His coat." She ran up to the car again. "Please, he needs his coat." But the door slammed shut, and they drove away.

She stood beside Frau Kramer at the end of the path. The taillights had long since disappeared, the sounds of the engine fallen silent. The deserted road seemed to lead toward an even deeper darkness, and Frau Kramer, clutching her son's coat, stroked the woolen fabric gently, as if she could feel her son within this outer shell.

She did not seem to realize that it was just his coat until they were back in the house, and then she collapsed on the sofa, weeping.

"A misunderstanding," said Therese in an effort to calm her. As she said the words, a band tightened around her chest, an undefined fear that went far beyond the word *misunderstanding*. She ran into the hall and telephoned Leonard's father at his chambers in Kleve. Then they waited.

How long did they sit there in silence? Ten minutes? Thirty? Or was it hours? In her memory it was an almost unmoving picture, etched in her head like a photograph, and, as in a photograph, time stood still. Frau Kramer's chest was the only movement, rising and falling with her tremulous breathing.

When they heard Herr Kramer's car, they both leapt to their feet and ran to the door. He was standing on the path, three or four steps away from the front door. With the key in his hand, he glanced at his wife, shook his head, and looked down. He was hatless, his coat muddy.

They had not told him what Leonard was accused of. When he insisted on his rights, and mentioned that he was there as his son's lawyer, they had seized him and thrown him out. He had fallen over. Monday, they had said. The prosecutor would be there on Monday, and he could come back then. He had driven back to his office and telephoned the prosecutor at home. A maid had answered the telephone and asked him to wait a moment. Then she had come back on the line. "The prosecutor is not available. Not for the whole weekend," she had said.

Frau Kramer took her husband's coat, went into the kitchen with it, and tried to clean the patches of mud off with a cloth. She did not look up, intent on rubbing the black woolen fabric, as if she could remove the whole day along with the dirt.

Blind with tears, Therese had ridden home. Her cheeks burned like fire in the cold, and at the same time she felt frozen in a way she had never known before. It was a cold not from outside, but that her heart pumped into her head, hands, and feet.

It was not until Monday that she learned what Leonard was accused of. "Lewdness with a person of the same sex," the charge read. Herr Kramer had been issued "a warning from the people."

Had she thought of Hanna before that, or had the nature of the accusation steered her suspicion toward Hanna? She went over to the Höver farm that very evening. She found Hanna in the barn, feeding the cows. She had tied her hair back under a kerchief, and her pretty, round face was flushed with the effort despite the cold. She wore a dark blue apron and an old cardigan over her coarse woolen dress. For the first time, Therese took conscious notice of Hanna's suffering, seeing how she had let herself go since Jacob admitted to her that he did not return her love.

"Leonard," Therese said warily, "you know what he's accused of?"

Hanna did not interrupt her work, but went on loading hay into the troughs.

"Do you know who reported him?"

"Don't know," Hanna threw out, "but there must be something to it. Nobody says that kind of thing for no reason."

Therese gripped her arm tightly. "Did you . . . ?"

Hanna flung the pitchfork to the floor, prongs first; the short, harsh scratching sound mingled with the metallic clang of the cows' chains as their heads moved up and down.

"And what if I did?" asked Hanna, her head held high. "If it's not true, he has nothing to fear."

"You mean . . . Leonard and Jacob? You've . . . ?"

Hanna went back to her work. Then, suddenly, she shouted, "I saw them! I saw them at the lake!" And Therese heard a mixture of pain and anger; she heard Hanna's voice crack.

She went up to her and whispered, "Hanna, you have to go there and tell them it's not true."

"Never! Never!" she cried. Fear flared up in her eyes. "If you say anything, my father will kill me. But I'll never take it back. Never. It's the truth."

Now, beneath the rattling of the chains, there was a humming sound, distant and strange, and for the first time Therese felt this lurching sensation within, as if something she had been holding in equilibrium was about to break away.

She could not remember how she got home. Later, she sat on her bed, incapable of putting her thoughts in order, deaf and mute with helplessness. "Thou shalt not bear false witness." "Thou shalt not kill." The word *truth* shriveled up in her head, trembling, thin, and melting into nothingness.

The next day, she came home from the Kruse farm. Her father met her at the door. "Something's happened," he said quietly. A weak light fell from the kitchen window onto the yard; the moon was nearly full, and it made her father's face look unnaturally waxen.

Had she immediately thought of Leonard? She no longer knew. All she knew was that she had put her hands over her ears and that her father's voice sounded muffled. "Leonard has hanged himself," he said, and she hit out at him, shouting that he mustn't say that, that it couldn't be true.

Therese Mende got up from the sofa and closed the sliding door to the terrace. She tried to ignore the brief stabbing sensation in her chest. The wind had gotten up some more; the pounding of the breakers was audible inside the house. Luisa, busy in the kitchen, was humming as she prepared supper.

Leonard had torn his shirt into equal-length strips and hanged himself from the window grate in his cell. They had wanted names from him; if he told them who he had "done things" with, he could expect a light sentence, they had told old Kramer. He pleaded with his son, but Leonard remained silent.

The days after his death seemed frozen in the flat expanse, rigid with grief and shock.

The pastor refused to bury him in the cemetery. His father and Herr Kramer begged him, but he stood firm. "A suicide, and further-more someone who . . . No. Never in consecrated ground." His mother agreed with the pastor. She got down on her knees at her pew and prayed for the young, lost soul.

Using a pickaxe, they cut a hole in the frozen earth just outside the cemetery, next to the hedge. Herr and Frau Kramer, Therese and her father, Alwine and Frau Kalder, gathered for a small, unobtrusive ceremony. Jacob, who was in France, knew nothing of all this. Wilhelm had been contacted in Stuttgart, but he had not come.

Alwine spoke to her again for the first time that day. "Why isn't Hanna here?" she asked.

Because it's her fault, Therese wanted to say, but she replied, "I don't know." She had wanted to say, Just stay beside me. Tell me about your happy days in Cologne. Say this is all a bad dream.

The lurching in her insides, the sense of disorientation, made her remain silent.

Years later, she had been at an art exhibition in London with her second husband, Tillmann. A sculpture caught her eye: scorched logs, piled up on top of one another, that required an invisible spike, a kind of core, to stabilize them. The figure, apparently defying the force of gravity, stood upright on a granite base. The name of the artist was written on a small brass plate. Underneath, it said, "Inner Equilibrium."

She had felt it again there, this lurching sensation, and understood that her faith in the simple rules of her Catholic childhood had been lost that day.

Chapter 22

April 23, 1998

Karl van den Boom parked his car in the street, took his pistol out of the glove compartment, and walked the three hundred yards along the path to the cottage. As he approached, he saw that the lit-up window they had seen from the Höver farm was that of Rita Albers's study. He got off the path, followed the hedge around the boundary of the property, and opened the little gate at the end of the garden. Apple blossoms lay on the grass, glimmering in the darkness like freshly fallen snow.

Van den Boom unbuttoned his jacket. It was tight across his shoulders and restricted his movements. For a moment, he asked himself whether what he was doing was wise, and whether he ought really to report his whereabouts to the dispatcher in Kleve. Then he edged over to the front of the terrace and looked over the balustrade. A man was standing by one of the shelves with his back to the window, apparently busy with a file. He was wearing a gray jacket over his jeans, and he was unusually tall.

Van den Boom ducked his head down, muttered "Shit!" and went around the terrace to the front of the house. His Homicide colleagues' blue car was in the drive, just behind the carport.

Hurriedly, he put the gun in his jacket pocket, buttoned up the jacket, and rang the doorbell.

His colleague Brand showed himself at the kitchen window for a moment, then opened the front door.

Karl van den Boom greeted him briefly. "Saw a light and thought I'd better take a look."

Brand, known to one and all as "the Long One," nodded. "I thought maybe we'd overlooked something." He sat down at the desk and looked at Van den Boom. "You live here, don't you?" he said pensively. "What's the story with this Peters? What's behind it?"

Karl shrugged. "Have you read the files?"

The Long One, eyes narrowed to slits, said acidly, "Yes, just after you did."

Van den Boom held his gaze eye and rumbled, "Hmm . . . Don't really see what anyone can say about that. I thought maybe I'd have a word with Gerhard . . . Ask why they closed the file after only two months." He did not mention the hint Paul Höver had dropped.

The Long One burst out laughing. "If anyone's going to talk to Gerhard, it's us. You keep yourself—" His words were interrupted by the ringing of the telephone. After the third ring, the answering machine clicked on. A man's voice spoke. "Hey, Rita, it's me. Wanted to hear how far you'd gotten with the Peters story. Call me . . ."

The Long One grabbed the receiver. "Hello." Silence fell at the other end of the line. Van den Boom pressed the "Speaker" button, and the Long One frowned with irritation. "Hello, who's speaking?"

"That's what I'd like to know," came the response from the other end, after a short pause. "That's Rita Albers's line, after all."

"This is the police," Brand replied. "And now I'll ask again: whom am I speaking to?"

Van den Boom turned the telephone toward him. The display said "Thomas." He pointed this out to the Long One.

"Where's Rita?" came from the receiver, which was now lying on the blotter as the Long One made a note.

"Frau Albers is dead."

The "Good God!" came immediately, and the reaction was genuine.

"Look . . . Thomas. Tell me your full name and what you have to do with Frau Albers."

"Was she . . . Was she murdered?"

"What makes you say that?"

The other person hung up. Brand slammed his open hand down on the desk and leapt to his feet. "What an asshole! Does he think we're stupid, or what?" He went through the telephone's address book and noted down the number. He reached for the receiver, but Van den Boom held him back.

"No, no," he rumbled calmly. "Let's give him a couple of minutes to think it over."

The Long One was about to make a retort, but he thought better of it. Two minutes later, the telephone rang again, and Van den Boom grinned with satisfaction.

It was Thomas Köbler. "Look, I'll make a deal with you. You keep me updated on this case, and I tell you what I know. I'm in Düsseldorf right now, so I could be with you in, say, an hour and a half."

The Long One was about to tear him off a strip, but Van den Boom snatched up the receiver and said, neutrally, "In an hour and a half, at the police station here in Kranenburg. That suits us fine."

He hung up.

He smiled benevolently at his young colleague.

"Always best to take one step at a time," he said slowly. "Let's let him come here first. Then we'll form an opinion. I mean, if this really is about that story from fifty years ago, a couple of hours now won't make any difference."

Chapter 23

April 23, 1998

Robert Lubisch had called his friend Michael Dollinger that afternoon. By the time Robert arrived, the lawyer had a bottle of the fin-
est Rioja and was studying the menu at a corner table in Brook, the
restaurant. They had shared an apartment for a long time as students,
and although they could not have been more different, they had soon
become friends. Michael was one of those men who was easy to over-
look, and as his life went on, he had learned to turn this fact to his
advantage. His was one of the largest legal practices in Hamburg. A
business with no headlines and no sensational cases. An address trusted
by Hamburg's elite.

Once Robert had sat down, Michael put the menu aside and
examined his friend critically. "You look like shit," he said bluntly as he
poured Robert some wine. "Now, tell me everything, from the beginning. What you told me on the phone left me none the wiser."

Robert laughed bitterly. "I can hardly believe it myself."

The waiter came to take their order three times in the next
twenty minutes, but he had to go away again each time, his mission

unaccomplished. Robert told his friend the truth about what had happened, beginning with his discovery of the papers and ending with the police's visit at noon.

When he had finished, Michael pushed the menu over to him. "Let's eat something," he said dispassionately, lighting a cigarillo. Once they had ordered, he leaned forward. "You think you're suspected of murder? Have I understood correctly?"

Robert gulped. Expressed so clearly, it seemed monstrous, but it was true. "Yes." He ran his hand over his face. "The officer told me to remain at his disposal."

Michael made a dismissive gesture. "That doesn't mean a thing. I mean, what motive are you supposed to have? I can take care of it, but I don't think you need to worry." He looked at Robert with his honest eyes and winked encouragingly. "They're checking you out, because you were probably the last person to see her alive. It's normal." He paused for a long while. "You know what I find much more interesting? Why you suddenly stopped being interested in the search for the woman."

Robert answered him directly. "Because she was this Peters's wife and not—as I suspected—some earlier lover of my father's. I didn't want to know any more than that." He thought for a moment. Then he corrected himself. "It's like this: I don't know what happened back then, but I know it probably wasn't what my father told me."

"And you're not curious?"

Robert shook his head. "No," he said vehemently. "Not anymore."

Their appetizers arrived and they ate in silence. Robert was listening to the murmur of voices in the restaurant, the quiet laughter, and the bright clinking of glasses as a couple at a neighboring table toasted each other.

"This whole story threatens me," he said impulsively. "You know I never got on particularly well with my father, but now . . . the story of his escape was actually the only thing I knew about his past, and when Rita Albers found out it couldn't be true, well . . ."

Michael chewed his salmon roulade with relish. When it became obvious that Robert was not going to finish his sentence, he did it for him: "You thought, 'Who knows what else she might bring to light?' Or, better expressed, perhaps, 'If what my father told me is a lie, what else has he kept quiet about?'"

Robert took a deep breath and smiled uncertainly at his friend. "Yes, more or less . . . But then I think again: The papers of this Peters are crusted with blood. He was obviously lying on the battlefield, and maybe my father really did think he was dead. He was a young, frightened soldier who just wanted to get away. It may have been like that."

Michael agreed. "Of course it may have been like that. It probably was like that, and your father has nothing whatsoever to do with what came after. After all, this Rita Albers said she had found Therese Peters. So the woman exists somewhere."

They ate in silence again. Then Michael leaned back. "At your last meeting, all she said was that the Peters woman had married again?"

Robert tried to remember the conversation. He saw Rita Albers in front of him, her agitated fidgeting. Had she been afraid? No. She had been furious. Combative.

"I asked her what a story like this was worth, and she said, 'Yesterday it was still a local-interest story, but its value has risen considerably in the course of a day.'"

Michael wiped his mouth with a napkin, lit a new cigarillo, and blew the smoke out with a hiss. "Now, that *is* rather interesting."

Robert nodded intently. "And then, I think, she said Therese Peters's maiden name was Pohl or Pohle, and that she had remarried under that name. I hope I'm remembering this correctly, but . . . she said 1956—1956 in Frankfurt."

Michael raised his eyebrows. "Well, it's possible to find out."

Robert raised his hands defensively.

Michael snorted. "Come on, Robert. You know as well as I do that the uncertainty's going to bother you to the end of your days if you don't resolve it now. And I'm not a journalist, after all, dead set on a story, but your friend and, what's more, a lawyer. At least think about it."

He signaled to the waiter, and they ordered espressos.

Robert thought about how liberated he had felt when the sale of his parents' home was signed and sealed. That was only a few months ago. "A line drawn under it," he had said to Maren. "A late, but definitive, line." And now he was more preoccupied with the old man than ever; he was even placing himself in a protective position over him.

"Okay," he said at last. "Find out."

Chapter 24

1941/42

Leonard's parents moved in with relatives in northern Germany that spring, and it was as if the last witnesses of his existence traveled with them. Leonard, it sometimes seemed to her, had been buried deeper than most dead bodies, and the little cross was soon covered by the budding branches of the hedge.

Alwine had returned home at her parents' request. Her mother was overwhelmed by the running of the estate, and she was to support her. Therese had reached the end of her labor service and found a job in the offices of the Hoffmann shoe factory. Wilhelm was back too; now he was wearing an SS uniform and went everywhere with Hollmann. He was often to be found at the Kalder estate.

Therese was meeting up with Alwine regularly again, and she took care to avoid encountering Wilhelm. Although Alwine was part of her old, carefree life, and they often laughed together again, they were unable to regain their earlier intimacy. They did not talk about either Wilhelm or Leo. It was on a rainy Sunday in May, as they stood by the window of the small parlor of the Kalder house—Jacob had written to announce a short visit on home leave—that Alwine first told her: "Jacob doesn't know."

Therese looked at her in disbelief. "Jacob doesn't know Leonard is dead?"

"Yes, of course he knows that." Alwine avoided her eyes. "But the other thing, he doesn't know that."

"But what did you . . . ?"

"That he killed himself," she said defiantly. She reached for Therese's hand. "Therese, it won't bring Leo back to life, and Jacob would . . . You know what he's like. Mother's afraid he would create difficulties for himself, and I beg you—in her name too—don't tell him it happened in prison." She smiled. "Do it for love of Leonard. So that Jacob has a good memory of him."

The rain was falling in soft, vertical threads, collecting in sand-brown puddles in the yard and raising bubbles that danced on the surface for seconds at a time and then burst.

"But he's sure to ask," she whispered. "He'll ask where he took his own life, and why."

And Alwine narrated a perfectly constructed story for her. Leonard had hanged himself at home. He had been unable to embark upon his studies because he was still unwell. This had depressed him greatly. Nobody knew what he had written in his letter to Jacob, but one could be sure he wouldn't have wanted to worry his friend. Alwine whispered conspiratorially, "I've discussed it with Hanna and Wilhelm. They agree it's for the best."

It was an absurd moment. She stared out of the window and felt as if she could see Leonard in the distance and hear him say, "That we promise, here and now, never to lose sight of each other, and always to be there for the others." She fought back her tears, unable to explain to Alwine how pernicious the lie was without giving Hanna away.

Hanna, screaming inside her head, "If Father finds out, he'll kill me."

Leonard, who had chosen to die rather than betray Jacob.

And now this lie.

It took her several minutes to understand that both Alwine and her mother also knew, or at least suspected, whom Leonard had been protecting.

She shook her head in disbelief, wanting to say, We can't do this, but Alwine beat her to it. She said, "Don't you understand? Jacob will do something stupid. You know what he's like, after all. They'll arrest him. He might do himself in too. Is that what you want?"

Therese Mende got up from the sofa. The pain in the left side of her chest had gotten worse. She went over to the sideboard, poured herself a glass of water, and took one of her heart pills. The light went on out on the terrace. Luisa had come out of the kitchen and was gathering together the cushions that had been swept off the chairs by the wind.

First the silence, then the lies. The one resulted, as a matter of course, from the other. Always.

Even at home, the tone had changed. Her mother now went to church twice a day, silently distancing herself from her husband and daughter. She could not bear the remoteness of the cottage, and she tolerated their modest circumstances with difficulty. "God's punishment," she would say, kneeling at the pew for hours and begging for forgiveness. Sometimes she would say, "God's will," and her father would leave the house in a rage.

Preparations for the invasion of Russia were in full swing, and Jacob's home leave was reduced from a week to two days. He visited her only once, for an evening walk. They went out among the fields and meadows, and the rich green, dotted with the yellow of dandelions, seemed to give the lie to that winter's events. She was distracted, fearful of his questions. He was thin; his face bore dark shadows. As if of their own accord, their steps led toward the cemetery, and she knew she would be unable to lie to him in front of Leonard's grave. He said, "If I ask you what happened, will you at least tell me the truth?" There it was again, this word, its single syllable ringing out so pure and so far.

She nodded. But he did not ask. He pushed aside the branches of the hedge behind the plain wooden cross and said, "Leo's father wrote to me." On the way back, he said, "I've volunteered for the Eastern Front." She did not ask why. She did not want to hear his answer. In the yard of the Höver cottage, he said good-bye and asked, "Do you know who denounced him?" She avoided his eyes. He raised his head and looked over at the Höver farm. "Why only him? Why not me?" he whispered.

Because she loves you, she wanted to say. Because she thought it was Leonard who stood in the way of her love. But she said nothing. Once again she saw Hanna that evening in the barn, heard her talk about truth too. As Therese and Leonard parted, he took her in his arms. "Take care of yourself," he whispered in her ear. Not "See you soon," not "Good-bye," and she did not want to hear the decision behind his "Take care of yourself."

Then he left.

Even today she could see him going. His head bowed, his arms dangling so helplessly from his shoulders. He did not turn around once.

The news came soon, in September. Frau Kalder's mouth quivered between grief and pride as the telegram was handed to her. "Fallen for the Führer, the people, and the fatherland," and the innocuousness of the word *fallen* took root in her mind. Over and over again, she saw him walking along the path, saw him fall and get up, fall and get up, fall.

Years later, she decided it was this telegram that rendered his death pointless.

When Hanna found out, she screamed like an animal in its death throes. Old Höver called for Dr. Pohl because she kept beating her head against the stable wall and he feared for her sanity.

Chapter 25

April 23/24, 1998

When he arrived at the police station in Kranenburg, the Long One dialed the Düsseldorf telephone number. He reached the editorial offices of a newspaper, and a young woman informed him that Thomas Köbler was on their staff, but he had left the building half an hour before. Van den Boom entered the name in his computer, but the man was probably an upstanding citizen because there were no results in the police database. They waited two hours, during which Van den Boom's young Homicide colleague paced up and down in front of his desk like a caged animal, cursing to himself. All this left Van den Boom, who had taken off his jacket and clasped his fingers over his belly, unmoved. Tomorrow was Friday, his day off. So he would be able to ask around undisturbed. First he would visit this Gerhard, and then he would go to the municipal archives. Frau Jäckel had told him she directed the Albers woman there. He would have loved to ask Brand what he knew about this Dr. Lubisch, but he would do better to call Homicide in the morning and talk to someone who was less furious with him.

After another hour—Thomas Köbler was still not at the newspaper, and it was past one o'clock in the morning—the Long One told Van den Boom angrily that he had interfered far more than he should, called him a provincial flatfoot, and left the police station, slamming the door shut with a bang.

Van den Boom leaned over his desk, pulled out his notebook, wrote *Thomas Köbler, Gerhard,* and *municipal archives.* Then he too gave up waiting, put on his jacket, switched off the light, and walked out to the parking lot. The night had cooled down by now, and he stood still for a moment, breathing in the clear air and enjoying the quiet. He set off at a stroll. His home, which he shared with his cats, Lili and Marlene, was only a few minutes' walk away.

He had put a good fifty yards behind him, when a car turned into the narrow street and raced past him. He recognized the Düsseldorf plates immediately, and ran back toward it. Thomas Köbler was about to get back in by the time he reached the parking lot.

"Herr Köbler?" he called out breathlessly.

The man looked young, and Van den Boom was not sure whether he actually was, or whether his shoulder-length hair and denim jacket just made him look it.

Köbler apologized for being late. An accident on the A57 had held him up for an hour.

Van den Boom unlocked the door and offered him coffee. He looked markedly older in the neon light.

Köbler accepted, thanking him, and looked at his interlocutor. "Was it you I talked to earlier on the phone?" he asked suspiciously.

"Me and my colleague," he said, nodding, as he got the coffee machine going.

Thomas Köbler did not seem interested in the question anymore. "So," he said, getting right to the point, "what happened with Rita?"

Van den Boom looked at him carefully. "Sit down," he said. "Let's begin at the beginning."

The man sat in the chair for barely two minutes, then leapt to his feet and began pacing up and down, like the Long One. The heels of his shoes clicked on the tile floor at each step, like a timepiece's second hand in a hurry. "I told you on the phone. I won't tell you anything unless I get something in return."

Karl closed his eyes in irritation. "I can tell you one thing for sure: you'll wear your shoes out if you go on racing about like that," he growled. He wiped his face and heard the bristles scrape. The sound made him feel momentarily tired. "How did you know Rita Albers?"

Köbler, who had sat down again, shrugged. "Three years ago, we worked together on a story about the murder of the then–prime minister of Bulgaria. After that, we were in touch only irregularly. I've obtained information for her occasionally, and vice versa."

"And Rita Albers asked you to obtain information about Therese Peters?"

Köbler crossed his arms across his chest. "It doesn't work like that," he began, with a show of self-confidence. "I want to know a few things first."

Van den Boom thought briefly. "Do you know Therese Peters's current identity?"

Köbler remained obstinate.

Van den Boom sighed. "Herr Köbler, if the death of Frau Albers is connected to the Peters case and you're stupid enough to make the same mistake as she did, then you'd better get off home as quickly as possible. I've been in charge here for eighteen years, and in that time there have been two drug-related deaths and one crime of passion. Go and die in Düsseldorf, please, and don't screw up my statistics."

The journalist looked at him in disbelief. He asked, "How do you know one is connected to the other?"

"I don't know," Karl van den Boom replied. He fetched two cups, placed them on the desk, and went on. "But I'll show I'm willing to meet you halfway. Frau Albers was bludgeoned to death. Her laptop, and probably some files, have disappeared."

Köbler nodded. "Anything else?"

Van den Boom waited. He pushed milk and sugar across the desk. "So," he said, as if ending the conversation, "it's late, and I've been off duty for hours. It's your turn to give me some information, but if you don't want to stick to the rules of the game, I suggest you drink up your coffee and get on your way."

Köbler's forehead creased in a frown. He held his cup in both hands. Van den Boom shut down the computer and switched off the coffee machine.

"I'll stay," said Köbler with emphasis. "How Rita died we'll probably be able to read in the papers tomorrow morning. That's not the information I wanted."

Van den Boom sat down again. "What information did you have in mind?"

"Rita must have found something explosive in Therese Peters's history, apart from her identity. And you know what."

Van den Boom was tired. He wrote the telephone number for Homicide on a sheet of notepaper and passed it across the desk. "Call them tomorrow morning," he said evenly, hoping Köbler would come up against Brand. He was surly and wouldn't let him off easily. After all, he was withholding important information for the solving of a crime.

Chapter 26

1942/43

She hardly ever saw Hanna; when they did meet, they said hello briefly and avoided looking each other in the face. Her visits to the Kalder estate became less frequent. Wilhelm was there almost every day, with the obvious intention of meeting her. He was often accompanied by SA Corporal Theo Gerhard, from Münster. A man with a soft, plump body and a loud voice that seemed at odds with his physique, he made even a polite request sound like an order.

Alwine was well aware of Wilhelm's intentions, and Therese would leave when his car entered the yard or turn back if she saw it already there. They did not discuss Jacob's death. Alwine wore black and had not yet rediscovered her former gaiety. She would wrinkle her nose and throw her head back in laughter, but there was something forced about her cheerfulness. Occasionally she would say, unprompted, "Everything will be fine, you'll see." And she would drive the doubt from her voice with a determined nod.

Therese's father had been working at the hospital in Bedburg-Hau since the summer. He was often away from home for days at a time.

At night, the wailing of sirens blended with the rumble of bombers. They kept coming, flying over the lower Rhine on their way to targets in the Ruhr, where they dropped their payloads onto the big cities. The colors of the summer crept past her weary eyes and turned into fall, and in September an army truck delivered some Russian prisoners of war, labor for the fields. Four men were allocated to the Kalder estate, two to the Höver farm. As the SS squad leader in the town hall, Wilhelm was responsible for the work and for supervising the Russians. He patrolled the farms regularly, with SA Corporal Gerhard. Notices in the village warned against contact with the enemy and threatened severe penalties.

In the early days, as Therese rode to work in Kleve first thing in the morning, she would see the Russians already at work in the fields of the Höver farm. They would watch her go by, and she would pedal faster, frightened.

A scant few days later, on a Saturday evening, little Paul came running in. "The doctor must come. The Russian is dying." Her father packed his bag and asked her to come with him. In a corner at the back of the barn, there was a partitioned area with two narrow cots against the clapboard wall. A kerosene lamp hung from a beam, shedding a diffuse light. The sick man lay curled up on one of the cots; the acrid smell of vomit wafted from a bucket beside him. Dr. Pohl turned the man toward him. His face was battered, and there was a gaping wound in his forehead. He pulled back the blanket. The thin body was covered with bruises.

He spoke soothingly to the man. "Why did he do this?" he asked. The answer came from the rear of the shelter. They had not noticed the man there, leaning motionless against the clapboard wall. "He had a fever," he said, stepping out of the shadows. Tall and thin, his face unshaven and cadaverous, his dark hair shoulder length, his clothes filthy and too big for him. He rolled the words around in his mouth, making them round and heavy. His upright posture lent him an air of pride that refused to accept the rest of his appearance.

Therese Mende looked at her watch. It was well after midnight; Luisa had gone home long ago. The wind had let up and rain was rattling down, setting off the motion detectors on the terrace so that they lit up and illuminated everything. She stood up and watched as the water formed a reflective surface on the paving stones and was pierced, bullet-like, by each succeeding round of raindrops.

Was that the night it happened? She no longer knew. She had wanted him to go on speaking forever, forming those words that trundled across the barn like earthen bullets. "Herr Höver says Fedir sick," he went on carefully, "and should rest. Not work."

She felt ashamed, because she had thought Höver had done this to the man, and she saw her father breathe a sigh of relief too. "Herr Höver was with me in field. Peters and Gerhard came. Hanna fetched us." He fell silent and stepped back into the shadows. She thought, *Wilhelm didn't do this. It was Gerhard.*

Her father sent her back to the house. "Hot water," he said, "and something we can use for dressings." Hanna was standing in the kitchen. She had boiled some water and torn a bedsheet into equal-sized strips. "What else do you need?" she asked, the harshness in her voice not matching the care she had taken. She looked up only once, briefly, clenching her teeth together to hide the quivering of her chin.

Therese and her father both nursed Fedir, who kept whispering the name "Yuri" and reaching for his friend's hand. Yuri. Twice she came close to him. He smelled of sour sweat, earth, autumn air.

Her father asked where he had learned to speak such good German. He said his mother came from a family of immigrants and had taught him. She thought she saw a brief smile. He went on to say he had been an architecture student, and it sounded as if it had been in another life. "Fedir is only . . . seven-and-ten," he explained quietly, and she was happy at this number, which sounded so strange and yet so right.

Hanna brought a dish of cabbage soup, placed it on the wooden chest, and turned to leave.

"Hanna." Dr. Pohl held her back. "Where's your father?"

Hanna turned, hesitating. "He was going to the town hall," she said tonelessly. She looked at Yuri and scolded him. "The cows need to go back to their meadows, and the potatoes need to be bagged up." Her voice cracked. "I can't do it all by myself!" she cried, and ran over to the house.

Yuri set to work immediately. Therese fed soup to Fedir, and her father followed Hanna into the house. A few minutes later, he set off for the town hall, but old Höver met him on his way back. "Won't happen again," the old man said in his brusque way. "Not on my farm."

It was not until years later that Therese would learn why old Höver was so sure.

Fedir had a high fever, his dressings needed changing hourly, and somebody had to make sure he got enough fluids. Therese's father and Höver carried him along the path to the cottage in a handcart. Therese's mother tried to stop them, wailing, "We'll all be thrown in prison." For the first time in her life, Therese saw her father angrily rebuke her mother. Old Höver stood there with his cap in his hand, just like that time in their old house. "Frau Pohl," he said respectfully, "I promise you nothing will happen. And it's only until the lad gets over the fever." Fedir stayed, and her mother nursed him. At first she did it reluctantly, but when she discovered a small crucifix hidden in Fedir's hand, her reservations seemed to vanish.

Wilhelm came to check the Höver farm from time to time, but now he came without Gerhard. He would ask Hanna or old Höver if everything was all right, then drive away. He did not enter the partitioned area in the barn.

Yuri visited Fedir every evening, and Therese rode home quickly after work in order not to miss him. When he left, she would go outside with him. Although the nights were cold, they would stand on the path and talk for a long time. Sometimes he would search for words, and she would find and offer them to him, and he would accept them like small gifts. Once she slipped on the muddy path, and he caught her. She looked deep into his brown eyes for only a few seconds, but she felt a new and unfamiliar life stirring within her, like an airy dance.

Fedir stayed with them for ten days. When he went back to the Höver farm, Yuri no longer had an excuse to come to the cottage, and from that day on they met at the edge of the forest and walked in the shelter of the trees, always watchful in case someone spotted them.

Therese Mende remembered what it had been like, the first time she stroked his face. Höver had gotten him a straight razor, and Fedir had cut his hair. She had run her fingers through the thick, crudely trimmed mop of hair, and then she could not leave him alone. She caressed his cheeks, ran her hand over his forehead, traced the dark eyebrows, and stroked the thin lips. He pulled her to him. Later, she thought she had stood like that for hours. The warmth of his caressing hands penetrated the cloth of her jacket; it was like a summer's breeze on naked skin, opening up pathways to her innermost self, and everything in her felt driven toward him. They kissed. When they let go of each other, she felt invulnerable to the chill of the evening. He whispered, "This can't be," and took a fearful step back. She knew it. She could see the posters in front of her, warning against contact with the enemy, but inside her there was only this unfamiliar desire, this energy, pulsing like waves, and a joy she had never known before, sweeping away all doubt.

Wilhelm ran into her a few days later as she was fetching her father's shoes from the cobbler's. He was waiting by her bicycle and said, with a slightly reproachful tone, that she had not been seen much lately. She talked about a lot of work at the company, her father hardly ever being at home, and the gardening, which now fell to her and her mother. She slung her shoes, tied together by the laces, over her shoulder and reached for the handlebars. "I could pick you up on Sunday," he suggested. "We could go for a ride along the Rhine, or into town. Surely you need to see something different occasionally."

"That's sweet of you, but I really have no time," she said hurriedly, pulling the bicycle toward her. Wilhelm gripped the saddle and said quietly, "Therese, I . . ." He grabbed her arm. "Can't we at least meet up every now and then?" She looked down, shaking her head. "No, Wilhelm. That wouldn't be good." His voice changed. "Is there someone else?" The sharpness of his tone startled her. For a moment, she thought, *He knows.* Her heart started pounding with fear. A bitter smile played about his lips, and he asked quietly, "Is it someone from the factory?"

She hid her relief.

Therese Mende opened the terrace door. The rain had slackened; the glimmerings of dawn painted a slender, pale gray edge onto the still-turbulent, night-dark sea. During the course of the next few hours, the remaining clouds would migrate across the island, and by midday at the latest the sky would be blue again.

How stupid she had been. Wilhelm's question had seemed like a sign from fate, and she had confirmed his suspicion. She had believed he would give her up if she was no longer available. She had said, "Yes, someone from the factory."

Chapter 27

April 24, 1998

Karl van den Boom had slept badly, and at six o'clock he shuffled down to the kitchen to make himself some breakfast. Lili rubbed herself against his legs, while Marlene lay curled up on a cushion on the windowsill, fast asleep. As usual, he talked to Lili. "If the municipal archives open at nine, I should be able to reach Schröder at home at eight, shouldn't I? What do you think?" The cat now added the feeding bowl to her circuit, tracing regular figures-of-eight around legs and bowl, while Marlene opened her green eyes from time to time and then immediately closed them, bored.

The scent of coffee spread. He put two slices of bread in the toaster, placed jam, butter, and cheese on the table, and brought in the newspaper. Rita Albers's death was the lead article in the local section. The headline read, "Woman Found Dead in Country House." Karl laughed mockingly. "Oh, Lili, they have to exaggerate everything. Now even a cottage is a country house." In his article, the reporter speculated it was a break-in gone wrong. So Karl's Homicide colleagues had not released any information.

On the dot of eight, he picked up the telephone and called Schröder, the archivist. The man had heard rumors the previous evening. "But . . . for God's sake, I didn't know it was that journalist."

He explained what Rita Albers had been investigating. "My impression was that her interest lay in the death of Wilhelm Peters and the suspicion hanging over his wife. So do you think her death . . . that this research had something to do with it?"

Van den Boom reassured him. "No, no. We're just trying to reconstruct what Frau Albers was working on."

Schröder then recited from when till when Rita Albers had been with him, which documents he had shown her, and what questions she had asked. Van den Boom was impressed by the man's capacity for recall. He was about to leave, when Schröder added something else: "Maybe it's not important, but it seemed to me that she reacted with great excitement when she learned that a duplicate of Therese Pohl's birth certificate had been issued at the end of 1952. The document wasn't mailed out, so it must have been picked up on-site."

Van den Boom brought the conversation to a close, pondering whether he should tell his colleagues that Köbler had come the previous evening after all and would report to them during the day. He opened a can of cat food and filled the two feeding bowls. Now Marlene was wide awake too. "Ach, they'll soon notice him when he turns up," he rumbled quietly to himself, poured himself a last cup of coffee, then contentedly watched the cats eating.

Half an hour later, he was on his way to Kleve.

Theo Gerhard lived in an area of six-story apartment blocks. His apartment was on the second floor, and the door was buzzed open a few seconds after Van den Boom pressed the doorbell. He was climbing the first few steps, when a head appeared over the banister and barked down at him, "Who are you? What do you want?"

"Van den Boom," growled Karl. He shouted upward, "I'm a police officer. But maybe I should come up first—it'll be easier to talk."

When he reached the second floor, he found before him a man whose cheeks and nose were purple with burst blood vessels. Bushy eyebrows made his expression look somewhat dull-witted. "A colleague? So what is it?" The old man made no move to go into his apartment; he seemed determined to discuss the matter on the landing.

"It's about an old case you handled, which may have something to do with a current case. In other words, I need your help," said Karl ingratiatingly. Gerhard nodded complacently and now made a move toward his front door. "Well, come into my parlor then," he shouted, and Van den Boom did not know whether the man was hard of hearing or the volume was part of his self-importance. The living room was paneled in oak veneer, and the gray-green furnishings had seen better days. But throughout the place there was a cleanliness and order that irritated Van den Boom.

Gerhard sat down opposite him. He did not offer any coffee, which caused Karl mentally to dismiss him as a colleague. A man was entitled to expect a drop of coffee, after all.

With a condescending gesture, Gerhard told him to go ahead: "Go on then, shoot."

"Do the names Wilhelm and Therese Peters mean anything to you?" Karl asked. He noted that Theo Gerhard did not show the slightest surprise.

"The Peters case? Of course I remember. The woman was a murder suspect. Went underground."

"Correct. I've read the file."

"So you know."

"Well, yes, but the file is rather thin, and that's not just because of the lightweight paper. I was struck by the fact that it was closed only two months after Frau Peters disappeared."

Gerhard snorted derisively. "Yes . . . and so what? That's the way it was back then. Searching for a missing person was difficult, and God knows we had other things to do. Besides"—he drew his bushy eyebrows together in a frown—"our evidence was purely circumstantial." He paused, trying to read Van den Boom's expression.

"And why were you certain it was a murder?" asked Karl.

Gerhard looked him up and down, then leaned forward. "Wilhelm would never have just taken off, you see? He had no reason to. Besides, his family was sacred to him, and he would at least have told his parents."

Karl seemed absorbed in an examination of the tiled coffee table, stippled with morning sunlight filtered through white net curtains. He went on, casually. "Now a journalist who was taking an interest in the case, a woman, has been killed, and I ask myself whether there were other reasons to close the case."

The purple lines on Gerhard's cheeks seemed to darken a little, but that was only because the skin around them had turned pale. Karl went on. "I heard you were an old friend of Peters's. You were in the SA, and he was in the SS, after all."

Gerhard exploded. "What do you mean by that? Those were different times, and after the war, I went straight back into the police. Oh sure, that would have been possible if I'd had skeletons in my closet."

Van den Boom leaned back, crossed his hands over his belly, and played the part of the man misunderstood. "But, Herr Gerhard, I don't think any such thing. I just wanted to know, since you were friendly, what kind of people they were."

There was a pause. The old man sniffed hard, then got up and went over to the dresser. He put a bottle of brandy and two snifters on the table and poured. It was a little early for Van den Boom, but if it would make the old man more talkative, it was all right by him. He suddenly realized what had irritated him so much when he stepped into the living room. The room seemed so tidy because there was nothing to tidy. No personal items, no little bits of decoration, no knickknacks that might reveal an inclination in any particular direction. There was nothing on the windowsill. What he could see of the dresser was empty.

There were no framed pictures of friends or family, and on the coffee table, where the bottle and the two glasses now stood, there was only a TV guide. The home was silent about its occupant.

Gerhard sat down again. "Wilhelm and I were investigated as part of the de-Nazification process and cleared."

Cleared, thought Van den Boom. It sounded better, of course, than Schröder's "a follower, against whom nothing could be proved." But he said nothing and nodded understandingly at Gerhard. "And Frau Peters? What was she like?"

The old man made a dismissive gesture.

"She was a slut, if you want my opinion. Wilhelm was crazy about her. The love of his life. He didn't understand what kind of a person she was." He picked up his glass, drained it in one go, and put it back on the table heavily.

"During the war, she could make good use of him. That was why she married him. It had been touch and go for her father since the late thirties. Only managed to save his skin because he was a doctor, and his respectable little daughter had someone at the front and carried on with another one here. Wilhelm risked his career for that little slut; he was completely blinded by love. And once the war was over, she didn't need him anymore—he was a burden to her. He suffered like a dog, I can tell you." He poured himself some more, not noticing that Van den Boom had not yet touched his own glass, and went on. "And then, as if by magic, he disappeared in 1950, after she had had a loud argument with him at the Marksmen's Fair." He nodded to himself knowingly. "And a few weeks later she was gone."

Karl pushed his snifter to one side. It made a scratching noise, naked and harsh. He waited; he felt certain the old man had not finished. Gerhard sat leaning forward, elbows resting on his knees, perhaps absorbed in the old images. Then he said, "That journalist woman called me." He looked up. "Day before yesterday. But I got rid of her, told her I wouldn't talk to her."

Karl did not allow his surprise to show; he just nodded content-edly, as one does when one hears things one has been expecting.

"What did she want?"

"Don't know," Gerhard snapped. "I told her I wouldn't talk to her."

Van den Boom saw uncertainty in Gerhard's eyes, and he thought he knew what the problem was. Gerhard had been drunk, as he probably was routinely from midday on. He couldn't remember exactly.

Karl mentally went through his notes. He asked, "Did she mention the name Lubisch?"

The old man shook his head and thrust out his lower lip. "No. No, who would that be?"

Karl believed him. "I got a tip-off," he said, changing the subject, "that something to do with this Peters must have happened at the end of the war. I was told I should ask you about it."

Gerhard's heavy-lidded gaze became watchful. "That's enough." His voice, not loud anymore, hissed menacingly. "Clear out of here right now."

"What are you so worried about?" Van den Boom asked innocently.

"Out!" the old man bellowed, indicating the exit with an out-stretched arm.

Karl felt certain he would get no farther here. He heaved himself out of the armchair. At the door, he turned around again. Gerhard had remained seated and was staring ahead. "You know what I think? I think you were quite glad when Therese Peters disappeared and the file was closed so quickly, because you weren't interested in finding her."

The old man glanced into his snifter and did not move.

On the way back to his car, Karl decided to pay a visit to his colleagues in Homicide. Just to find out whether they had anything new. And maybe Köbler had been there.

Chapter 28

April 24, 1998

Michael Dollinger called Robert Lubisch at the clinic at ten o'clock.

"That was quick," Robert joked, firmly convinced that Michael had gone a little too far the previous evening and was now about to tell him the matter was more difficult than he had assumed.

Dollinger did not give him time to follow this train of thought for long. "Are you sitting down?" he asked.

It took Robert two seconds. "Have you found her?"

"I certainly have," came from the other end of the line, "and now it becomes clear why that journalist thought the story was worth money."

Robert waited tensely.

"Are you still there?" asked Michael Dollinger.

"Yes! Get on with it! Tell me."

"Does the name Mende mean anything to you?"

Robert Lubisch thought about it. "No. Is that her name now?"

Michael laughed. "The name would mean something to your wife. Maybe you've heard of Mende Fashion?"

"You mean the design firm?"

"The very one. Mende Fashion. Established in London in 1964 by Tillmann and Therese Mende. In 1983, they transferred the company to Germany. Tillmann Mende was the designer, responsible for creative matters, and . . ." Michael paused, then spoke the next words with relish. "His wife, Therese, née Pohl, whom he married in 1956, was the business brains. Today, the company has outlets all over Europe. Tillmann Mende died in 1995. One year later, his wife handed control of the company to their daughter and retired. She lives in Mallorca now."

Robert listened, his thoughts in turmoil. He had led Rita Albers to this. Had she threatened to expose Therese Mende?

"Hello?" he heard his friend saying at the other end.

"Yes, I'm just trying to get this in order. I mean, this would have been a full-blown scandal for this Mende woman. Do you think . . . ?"

"I don't think anything, but I have the address and phone number here, and I suggest you hand this over to the police. In any case, even if you did hit upon the story, you can assume the consequences have nothing to do with your father."

Robert wrote down the address and phone number. He took a deep breath. "Michael, I owe you one."

"Not for this. This was three phone calls, and I did it with pleasure."

Robert looked at the address he had copied into the space for the following day in his week-at-a-glance calendar. Saturday.

"Tell me, how did you find out so quickly?"

Dollinger laughed, then said something about trade secrets and how it was all about good contacts in his line of work.

They said good-bye to each other. Lost in thought, Robert stared at the entry. Maren would be in Brussels until the middle of next week. He was only on duty till noon today, and he was free on Saturday. He turned the page. There was nothing special on Sunday either, only the late shift.

He put off the call to the police till later. For the next two hours, he looked after his young patients, noting the scraps of thought rolling gently along beneath the routine. In the corridor he spoke to one of his colleagues and asked whether he could swap his Sunday shift with him. Quite spontaneously. It was not until he left his office at noon, having not called the police, with Therese Mende's address on a slip of paper in his breast pocket, that he admitted to himself that he had already made his decision during the telephone conversation with Michael Dollinger. He used a travel agent to book a flight for that evening, two nights in the place in Mallorca where Mende lived, and a return flight for Sunday evening.

At home, he searched the Internet for entries about Mende Fashion. He found photographs of Tillmann Mende and some later ones in which he was seen together with his daughter, Isabel. There was only one photograph of Therese Mende at her husband's side. It dated from 1989 and was part of a publication marking the company's twenty-fifth anniversary. He recognized the features immediately, and yet it seemed like another woman. The gaze that had so drawn him in his father's old photograph had disappeared. Here, a serious woman in a high-cut dress looked remotely, almost arrogantly, out at the camera.

Was it credible that this woman had removed Rita Albers from her path? He studied the picture for a long time and confessed to himself that he had made the arrangements for his trip because, thanks to the old photo, such a link had seemed unthinkable. Because he had thought his curiosity might have created some difficulties for the woman, and he ought to clear them up. But now?

He shook his head abruptly. Then he packed a travel bag. He took Peters's identity card, the safe-conduct pass, and his father's discharge papers out of his jacket pocket and added them to the contents of the bag. There was still another hour before he had to leave for the airport, when the doorbell rang.

The two police officers from before were standing at the door. They needed his fingerprints. "Routine," said Söder. He licked his lips. "It's just to distinguish your prints from others," the woman explained. He was glad she was the one who pressed his fingers onto the ink pad and then the paper.

He did not say anything about Therese Mende and his travel plans. On the way to the airport, he decided to call Dollinger from Mallorca. Just in case.

Chapter 29

1943

The winter of 1942/43 was icy. Old Höver brought Yuri and Fedir into the house in the evening and let them sleep on the kitchen bench. Wilhelm continued his checks on the Höver farm. He did not notice this breach of the rules on the accommodation of prisoners of war, but one day, at lunchtime, he found Yuri and Fedir eating with the Hövers. Wilhelm was beside himself. "You promised me you would abide by the rules. Eating with the enemy is forbidden." He roared at Yuri and Fedir, "Out into the barn! Or you'll be leaving here before you know what's what." Höver, unimpressed, said, "Stay where you are. We work together, so we can eat together." He turned to Wilhelm. "If you think I'm going to turn communist because I eat with one, I can set your mind at ease. I'm not a Nazi either, even though I've had dealings with you for years."

Yuri told her about it during one of their secret rendezvous. They met once or twice a week, stood clinging to each other tightly for half an hour, then parted, frozen through. That evening, at the end, he had fallen silent and then whispered, "Therese, I'm worried. We're a danger to the Hövers, to Fedir, and to your parents." When she considered their fear-filled secrecy, his phrasing seemed absurd to her. They were standing in the freezing cold, concealed and shivering, and yet they were a danger to others. He talked about not meeting anymore, and her heart raced. "Less often," she suggested, but after two weeks of seeing each other only once a week, they resumed their old routine.

These half hours with him kept her going; the days without him seemed lifeless; they were time she had to put behind her, like an obstacle between them.

He said, once, "When we haven't seen each other for several days, I'm afraid you don't exist, that I've only dreamed you."

She went to Heuer, the photographer, and smiled into the camera for Yuri and no one else. On the day after Christmas, in the evening, on the frozen lake, she gave him the picture. He lifted her up and whirled her through the air. They kept slipping on the ice, stumbling and catching each other. The night-black sky filled the gaps between the snow-covered trees. The twigs and branches glowed like a white spiderweb, shielding their high spirits. The only sound was the crunching of their shoes on the ice and, from time to time, a suppressed gurgle of joy.

They were like children with a secret zest for life, dancing to unheard music. Once a squadron of bombers rumbled overhead, pushing onward to where the war was. It was not here; it was far away. It could not be where they were.

Therese Mende sat in her armchair and felt weak. It was nearly noon already, and the sun was taking over the sky. Luisa had opened the sliding doors onto the terrace, and a light breeze filled one of the soft, cream-colored blinds. She called her housekeeper and asked for an espresso. She had missed her morning walk and wanted to make up for it.

Sometimes she did not think about the war for days at a time, but simply forgot it. And in that peace that belonged to them alone, they would stand wrapped up in each other, one body, one breath. Hands whispering, searching, insisting, under their coats. When they released each other in the small hours, it was like a tearing apart, and the days that followed, during which they could not see each other, heaped the hours, minutes, and seconds into great towers that seemed insurmountable.

And in the face of all the adversity, she had never in her life been so strong, with an energy that lifted her soul and carried all before it. Yuri told her once, "In my country we say, 'True love is a circle. It has no end.'" She accepted the saying like a pledge. Like an ancient, incontrovertible truth.

She went up to her dressing room.

When one is young, one has no idea that love persists, even when the other person is gone. Like a phantom pain. And then that pain is like a ring. It has no end.

In the factory office she had made friends with Martha and Waltraud, two colleagues of her own age. Waltraud's fiancé was at the front, and Martha flirted with every man who came into the office wing.

It was a Monday in mid-February. At lunchtime Martha asked her, "Listen, do you know Wilhelm Peters?" Therese was surprised. Martha told her she had met him at a dance that weekend. "He kept asking me to dance, but all he did was ask about you. Talked about you constantly, wanted to know who your lover was, claimed you were with someone from the factory." She pouted. "I think he's completely in love with you. So I don't stand a chance."

Therese choked back her feeling of sickness and asked cautiously, "What did you tell him?"

Martha laughed. "Well, that he needn't worry. If she had anyone in the factory, I said, I'd know about it."

Therese could hardly breathe, and Martha's voice sounded strange in her ears. "He's good-looking, that one, makes a good impression. I could go for him," she heard her say, and then it was just scraps of sentences: ". . . probably jealous . . ." and ". . . won't give up so easily . . ." and ". . . often standing by the factory gates . . ."

When they went back to the office, the metallic clattering of the twelve typewriters seemed to hammer at her, and she was unable to put together a single clear thought. She worked mechanically until the evening, and as she rode her bicycle home and felt the damp cold cooling her face and head, she slowly regained a sense of inner order. She had not forgotten Wilhelm in the last few weeks. Not Wilhelm. But his interest in her, which now felt like a curse. Her thoughts came thick and fast. Until now, he had thought his rival was to be found in the factory. Martha had seen him at the gates several times. Would he now start watching her at home too?

That evening she went to see Alwine, whom she had neglected in recent months. Her friend welcomed her in a friendly, almost effusive manner, and at first she was uncertain how to go about asking after Wilhelm without reawakening Alwine's old jealousy. But Alwine raised the subject herself.

She smiled conspiratorially. "So tell me," she said excitedly, "who is it?" Therese looked at her wide-eyed, not knowing how to answer. "Oh, come on," cried Alwine happily, "the sparrows are chirping it out from the rooftops. What's his name?"

The questions caught her unprepared, and when she began to lie, she saw suspicion on her friend's face. Therese lowered her head in embarrassment and asked, "What do they say?"

Alwine laughed with relief. It was her old, infectious laugh, and it brought back their previous intimacy. "More than anything else, people say you're making a big secret of it."

She thought it was important to Alwine that there was someone else, that she, Therese, was no longer within Wilhelm's grasp. And there was this overwhelming fullness inside her, this urge to share her happiness. She took her friend's hand. "You must never betray it," she whispered. "Promise me." Alwine's eyes opened wide and round, and Therese called to mind all the secrets they had shared and kept as schoolgirls. She told her about Yuri. When she said his name, Alwine put her hand to her chest. She said, "You mean . . . a Russian?"

Therese Mende remembered every detail of that moment; she felt, even today, how she had been gripped by fear, how her heart did not want to take the next step, and how her knees went weak.

But then Alwine stroked her cheek and said, "Of course, that explains why you're making a secret of it." She looked intently into Therese's eyes. "No one must find out, especially not Wilhelm."

Her relief was boundless. They sat together for two hours, whispering and laughing just like old times. It was Alwine, in her ingenious way, who suggested a solution. "The best thing is to confirm the rumor and say he's a soldier." And she went further: when they saw each other again two weeks later, she had made contact with a friend from her time in Cologne. "He's an officer in France. He's engaged, but one of his men has agreed to write to you regularly," she said, beaming. Therese held her breath, close to tears; she thought her friend, with her high-spirited approach to life, had called attention to her secret. Alwine reassured her. "I wrote that you needed to protect yourself against an admirer's unwelcome advances, and a lover on the front was the best way."

From then on, she received regular mail from France, and Alwine made sure Wilhelm found out about it. In one of his first letters, the soldier, a private, asked for a photograph. She could not afford a new one, and it did not feel right to give a stranger a copy of the picture that was intended for Yuri alone. In the New Year, she put it among the pages of the letter she wrote to thank him for his efforts.

Her clandestine happiness with Yuri seemed unthreatened. The mild evenings allowed her to meet up with him for as long as two hours, sometimes in the nearby forest, sometimes by the lake, and now in the fading light of day. That they were no longer surrounded by darkness was perhaps the greatest gift of that spring. Along with the bittersweet scent of the elderflower bushes, which they could almost taste, it was the colors, above all else, that gave them optimism.

The whispered news made its contribution too. Underneath the official bulletins on the radio and in the newspapers, beneath the shrieks of "total war" and "final victory," there was another flow of information that passed by word of mouth. "The war is coming to an end. The war is lost." Her father listened to the BBC at work, with his colleagues, and he knew how the front was changing. When she told Yuri about it, he crossed himself, gave thanks for the news, and covered her face with featherlight kisses. Then he pulled her toward him, and they did not dare to talk about the future. They sat close beside each other and willed peace to arrive. They sat close beside each other and feared peace.

Chapter 30

April 24, 1998

The Long One was not in. Manfred Steiner, with whom Karl used to go out on patrol as a young policeman, was sitting at a desk in Homicide. He greeted him with the words, "You've made yourself unpopular."

Van den Boom rubbed his balding pate and feigned remorse. "But Köbler came last night after all and was going to show up here today."

Steiner frowned. He was gaunt and wore his thick, now-gray hair short; he carried reading glasses on a cord around his neck and was in the habit of clacking his arms against each other the moment he sat down. "He didn't show up here, and he's taken leave from the editorial office for the next two days." Steiner stood up, went over to the coffee machine, and filled two cups. He held one out to Karl. "So, what did Köbler tell you?"

Karl shook his head. "He was stubborn, wanted to know what Rita Albers had found out about Peters. He's probably doing his own research now."

"You mean the suspected-murder case from the early fifties?" Karl nodded. Steiner opened up a file. "So . . . for the moment we're not assuming there's a connection. Even if Rita Albers found the Peters woman, there's nothing in the old file that could be awkward for her today. Even at the time, there was nothing to substantiate the charge. So why, nearly fifty years later, would she kill Albers?" He leaned back in his chair. "We're checking out Albers's ex-husband and her private life. It looks much more like something to do with a relationship. The head wounds are massive, and the perpetrator struck several times. I can't see an old woman as the perpetrator."

Van den Boom took a sip of coffee and wondered whether he should tell Steiner about his visit to Gerhard, but decided against doing so. It could only be a good thing if they investigated in different directions and did not get in each other's way. That gave him some breathing space. "Have you found out anything about the murder weapon?" he asked casually.

Manfred Steiner snapped the arms of his glasses together. "A meat hammer, aluminum, surface area two inches by just under three. Probably came from the kitchen; at least, there was a rack of kitchen utensils of the same material there."

"Hmm," rumbled Karl, "but you haven't found the thing."

The telephone rang. Steiner picked up the receiver. Van den Boom tried to glean something from his responses.

"In the archives? . . . No, he can't . . . I have it here, and it's part of an ongoing investigation . . . Then he can be so good as to come here."

When Steiner hung up, Karl grinned at him. "Let me guess: Köbler's in Kleve and wants to see the Peters file."

His colleague put on his reading glasses. "Could it be that you know more than you're telling me?"

Karl shook his head. "Nothing concrete, honestly. Just inconsistencies, but lots of them. Too many, if you get me?" He told him about Hanna and Paul, and now also about Gerhard and his reaction to the question about the last years of the war. As he laid out this information, he remembered again how Hanna and Paul had reacted to the name

Lubisch. "This Lubisch," he asked. "How come he was interested in the Peters woman in the first place?"

"Our colleagues in Hamburg interviewed him." Steiner leafed through his papers. "Here." He pushed a computer printout across the desk. It was a photograph of a young woman. Karl was surprised. The young woman was not pretty in the conventional sense, but in this picture she was beautiful. He remembered Gerhard's remark that she was a slut.

Steiner quoted extracts from the file: "'Lubisch has a private interest . . . Found the photo among his late father's papers and wanted to know who she was. There was a note about Photo Studio Heuer, here in Kranenburg, on the back of the photograph . . . which led him to Rita Albers.'"

Karl stood up ponderously, thanked Steiner for the coffee, and made to leave. "Karl." Steiner stood up too. "I suggest we keep each other informed." Van den Boom nodded with satisfaction. "If you keep the Long One off my back, it's a deal."

Steiner laughed. "Interesting. This morning he said to me, 'Just keep that small-town sheriff off my back.'"

As Karl was leaving the station, he thought about the expression "small-town sheriff." He saw John Wayne in a rocking chair on the porch, dozing in the sun, with his feet up on the balustrade. People said friendly hellos to him, and he put thumb and forefinger to the brim of his hat and said hello back.

Small-town sheriff was a fine thing to be called.

Chapter 31

1943

They saw each other less often in the summer. There was work to be done on the farms from early in the morning till late at night. The systematic bombing of the Ruhr had begun. American long-range bombers flew over the lower Rhine during the day; the British took over at night. Wailing sirens and rumbling in the sky became routine, and perceptions became reversed. Several hours of silence now felt somehow ominous.

They met on the edge of the clearing with the lookout tower where she had dropped off and picked up identity papers, four years before. The space formed a long green oval; an old copper beech with a substantial crown stood in the center. Ruby red against slowly fading blue. One Sunday afternoon was of that particular silence that seems to originate in some other reality. They clung to each other and wanted to stay so forever, lying wordlessly in the grass amid such peace. Hands, light as wings, aroused trembling and then powerful shuddering, and they wanted each other totally, clothed themselves in a naked summer skin, bridged the gaps of unfamiliarity. On the first night, she did not experience it, but later she did. A sensation of floating and rising, and she learned with astonishment that the peak came as she fell. And when she opened her eyes, the ruby red of the beech was always there, with the blue of the sky behind it. These were the colors of happiness.

Her parents accepted her evening walks. Sometimes, as she set off, her father would say, "Be careful, child." He said it quite casually, quite quietly, and with it he whispered a secret about the secret. The letters continued to arrive from the private in France, and she wrote back with the same regularity. Once he wrote, *One of my comrades found your picture. I told him you were my fiancée. They all envy me.*

On September 28, 1943, she went to the Höver farm, as she did every Wednesday, to fetch milk. Everyone was busy with the turnip harvest, and there was a trailer in the yard from which Hanna and Fedir were unloading turnips. Therese said hello and went on into the covered yard. As she was using a ladle to fill her little can, suddenly Hanna was standing behind her. Avoiding Therese's eyes, she pushed a few strands of hair that had fallen over her face back under her kerchief. "Wilhelm asked Father how often you come here in the evening," she said without preamble.

The ladle fell to the ground, and Hanna stared at Therese. She bent down, picked up the ladle, took the can from Therese, and filled it mechanically. "Be careful," she said warningly. She passed Therese the milk can and left the hall in a hurry.

Therese Mende paused on the top step of the short staircase that led between two cafés to the beach. The previous night's rain and wind had left the sea in turmoil. The water was still greenish brown, and seaweed lay drying in a broad line on the sand.

That evening, she had left the lid of the can on the floor, and the milk had repeatedly sloshed over the rim as she made her way back to the cottage. Tears ran down her face, and she talked herself into thinking she was crying because of the spilt milk, rejecting the premonition that this was the beginning of the end.

The days that followed were indistinct, and when she did remember specific images—she did not realize this until years later—they were gray, as if the color had drained out of her life that autumn evening.

The very next morning, at about six o'clock, Theo Gerhard and two Gestapo men came and picked her up. They took her to Kleve— her and her parents. Her mother was allowed to go home the same day. Her father after two days. They were reluctant to let him go, but he was a doctor, and people in high places had insisted on his release.

The gray walls of her cell, the gray blanket on the bare platform bed, the gray interrogation room, the gray and black uniforms. And above it all Theo Gerhard's loud voice, which seemed always to be shouting, even when he tried solicitously, almost pleadingly, to persuade her.

She repeated again and again that she had a sweetheart in France and that she knew Yuri only by sight. She had met him at the Höver farm, and she had seen him working in the fields from time to time.

Gerhard struck her in the face and yelled, "Bolshevist whore!" Then he sneered, "We'll put that Russian up against the wall anyway."

On the third day, he tossed a pile of letters onto the table, took one at random, and ordered her to read it out loud. She read: *"Dear Fräulein Pohl, Your photo came today, and at last I have an image of you. I am so grateful that our NCO has asked me to write to you regularly . . ."*

Father told her later that she was in jail for eight days, so it must have been on the fifth or sixth day that Gerhard placed another document in front of her: *". . . That I saw Therese Pohl with Yuri in the forest . . . that they have often met on the edge of the forest and that they have kissed each other . . .*" The name Paul Höver had been typewritten underneath.

"A child," she said. "A child who can't even read." Gerhard leapt to his feet, shouting, "Are you going to be impertinent now too, you lying whore?" He threw the photograph that she had given Yuri down on the table.

What happened could only have lasted a few minutes, but to her it seemed endless. He yanked her out of the chair by her hair and flung her against the wall. The pain in her head was dull. She felt her knees go weak, saw the bare concrete floor of the interrogation room coming toward her, thought it was rising and that that was impossible. Blows to the face and flecks of Gerhard's spittle and his bellowing. Inexplicable stabs of pain throughout her body. Breathlessness when he punched her in the belly. Arms held protectively over her head, she saw the black boots hurtling toward her, over and over again, and she smelled shoe polish and blood and then nothing.

She did not come to until she was back in her cell, where she vomited and soiled herself.

All of this was just momentary images, fragments she was never able to piece together into a whole, not even in the years that followed. What remained in her memory was being scared to death—a fear that rendered her mute and blind, and almost made her lose her mind.

She did not know how much time had passed when she was fetched from her cell during the night, shoved along a corridor, and thrown out a side door. In the pouring rain, she dragged her way to Martha, who lived below Schwanenburg Castle. Martha screamed out loud when she recognized her, then pulled her hurriedly inside her home. Darkness. Brief moments of consciousness. Martha washing her, Martha bandaging her head, giving her something to drink. The next day, her friend brought in an acquaintance of hers, who loaded Therese onto a horse cart and took her home.

Her mother's wailing is still in her ears, and then the pictures break off.

She had open wounds on her head, a concussion, several broken ribs, scratches and bruises all over her body.

Wilhelm visited her two days later and was beside himself with fury. He had known nothing of it at all. From him she learned that Yuri had been condemned to death by a summary court, but that the execution had not yet taken place. Fedir had been sent back to the camp at Münster.

She wept and pleaded, told him he could ask anything of her if he would help Yuri.

Tears glittered in his eyes as he said, "You know I'd do anything for you, Therese. But what are you thinking? Do you really think I could help him escape and he could come back to you?"

"Just let him live," she whispered. "That's all I want."

Wilhelm paced up and down in front of her bed, not saying anything; occasionally he would stop by the window, looking out pensively. Then he asked, "Will you be my wife?" She did not understand, thought her broken, aching head was playing tricks on her.

He sat down beside her on the bed and went on, now sober and rational. "Therese, I'm willing to risk my life for you. Gerhard shouldn't have hit you. So he owes me something. Maybe I can help this Russian to escape, but then he has to disappear from here immediately, do you understand?"

Oh, this sudden hope. Of course she understood that Yuri had to go away. But he would live. She gripped Wilhelm's hand gratefully, and he asked again, "Will you marry me?" She hesitated, heard that this was the condition. She nodded. If Wilhelm risked his life to save Yuri's, the price would not be too high.

Five days and nights went by. Wilhelm did not come. She went back to helping her mother with light housework, sometimes thinking, her heart pounding, that she had only dreamed Wilhelm's visit. Perhaps her heartfelt wish that Yuri might not die had led her to imagine the conversation.

And then October 16 came, a Saturday morning that blanketed the whole area of the lowlands in thick fog. It was shortly after eight when she went out to feed the two rabbits. She was standing at the well, pumping water into a bowl, when Hanna emerged out of the fog like a ghostly apparition. "Yuri has to leave," she said. "He wants to see you one more time." She said it quietly, and the fog seemed to muffle her voice even more. Slowly, Therese put the water bowl down on the wall of the well; it took her several seconds to understand. "Come on," Hanna hissed. She turned and walked away.

She followed. Her ribs hurt as she ran to catch up with Hanna. She had a thousand questions in her head, but she could not put them into words. She had only one thought: *He's alive. He's alive.*

They did not follow the path. Hanna led her across the meadows and cleared fields toward the Höver farm. She pointed at the barn. "By the wall at the back," she whispered, and disappeared.

He was standing, leaning against the wall of the barn. He crossed himself when he saw her and said, "God is on our side, Therese." A black eye, a makeshift bandage around his head, his left arm in a sling, split lips—she could guess what it might look like under his clothes. They clung to each other for several minutes without saying a word.

He whispered, "Therese, we don't have much time." He took her face in his hands. "What have you done?" At first, she did not understand what he meant. "Why are they letting me go?" he asked, and fear of her reply flickered in his eyes.

Therese Mende walked close to the water. The sand was firm here, and walking required less effort. She had only lied to him that one time, wanting the short time they had together to be untroubled. Hope is without logic. Hope is irresponsible.

The war—everyone said so, after all—would be over soon. Then Yuri would be able to come back, and she could go away with him. Yuri did not necessarily want to go home; he had said so several times. "It's no better there," he had said.

She stroked the familiar face and said, "I asked Wilhelm for help."

He pressed her close to him. In a whisper, he told her what had happened to him.

Gerhard had picked him up. "He produced a piece of paper saying he was supposed to bring me to Kranenburg for questioning." And she thought idiotic thoughts like, *So he was in jail nearby the whole time.*

There had been another prisoner sitting in the van. Halfway into the transfer, in an isolated place, the van stopped. Gerhard opened the door, took Yuri's handcuffs off, and said, "Get lost." Yuri had stood still, firmly convinced that Gerhard would shoot him if he ran away. Gerhard laughed. "Shitting yourself now, eh?" He closed up the van, left Yuri standing at the rear, and went back to the cab. He stopped there for a moment. "You have your whore to thank for this," he said with a grin. He grabbed his crotch and thrust his pelvis back and forth. Then he climbed in and drove off.

Therese reassured Yuri. "Gerhard's lying. Wilhelm helped because he's an old friend."

When they parted, there was a measure of childlike optimism alongside the pain of separation. Yuri was going to hide out in the forest and try to cross the border into Holland by night. He said, "As soon as I'm safe, I'll send word to you." When he hobbled off into the fog and disappeared, she was sure she would see him again. Not in the next few days, not in the next few weeks. But soon.

Chapter 32

April 25, 1998

Robert Lubisch had rented a car at the airport. It was a little after nine and dark by the time he reached the resort. The hotel was near the beach and furnished in an airy, Mediterranean style; it being early in the season, the staff was friendly and helpful toward the few guests. His room with a balcony gave onto the inner courtyard, where an unused kidney-shaped swimming pool glowed turquoise.

He decided to take an evening walk and look around the town. He wrote Therese Mende's address, but not her name, on a slip of paper and asked for directions at reception. The concierge smiled and said promptly, "Ah, you want Señora Mende. It's not far." He explained the route, and Robert strolled through the balmy evening air. The restaurants, cafés, and bars along the short promenade were still uncrowded. He went up some steps, leaving these establishments behind, and entered a narrow alleyway that led steeply uphill. "Señora Mende lives a little out of town, at the highest point," the concierge had said, and Robert walked up the hill. The one-story house looked unimpressive from the street. Going past the house and viewing it from the side, he saw the terrace lighting, which seemed to float over the sea. Only then did he realize that a second story had been built into the cliff. He stood there for a moment, lost in thought, and a woman carrying a basket came out of the house. She stopped at the wrought-iron gate, looked at him suspiciously, and asked him sharply, in Spanish, what he wanted. He had not planned on visiting Mende until the next day, and in any case he had wanted to inform Michael Dollinger first, but now he made a spontaneous decision. He approached the woman, introduced himself, and cast about for the few Spanish words he knew. Then he gave up and said, in German, that he would like to speak to Frau Mende.

"It's late," the woman said reproachfully.

Robert nodded. "Oh, it doesn't have to be today. But perhaps she has some time tomorrow."

The woman asked his name again and went back into the house. Ten minutes went by, and he was about to leave, when the door opened and she waved him in. She led him along a spacious hallway with four broad, sweeping, marble steps that led down into a large room. Fine antiques and plain, modern furniture mingled in an uncluttered way. A large picture window led onto a terrace, covered near the house and then open beyond it.

Therese Mende was sitting in a delicate Chippendale chair, wearing a sleeveless, dove-gray roll-neck sweater over light-colored trousers. She gave an impression of brittleness. Robert told her his name, but she did not react; she sat motionless and stared at him. He felt he was dealing with a confused old woman, and he momentarily regretted his trip. He was embarrassed by his curiosity, and his suspicions now seemed utterly ridiculous.

She stood up slowly and walked toward him, her posture very erect. "Please forgive me, Herr Lubisch. I didn't mean to be impolite." Her voice sounded hoarse, and the hand she held out to him was cool and bony. She cleared her throat and said, firmly and matter-of-factly, "So, what can I do for you?"

While on the plane, he had considered what he wanted to say to her, but now he felt unprepared and did not really know where he should begin. He decided on the direct route. "Frau Mende, I'm here because I've come across something that has to do with you. Does the name Rita Albers mean anything to you?"

He could not discern any movement in her face. She remained silent for several seconds, then pushed a strand of her chin-length gray hair behind her left ear and asked, "May I offer you something? A glass of wine, perhaps, a whiskey . . . or would you rather have coffee?" He chose white wine. She took a woolen shawl from the back of the chair, draped it over her shoulders, and invited him outside. There were two wicker chairs at the end of the terrace. He had not been mistaken. The surface rested, platform-like, on a rocky outcrop from the cliff. The unhindered view of the bay and sea was impressive. They stood there in silence, listening to the gentle, regular rolling of the waves far beneath them.

The Spanish woman placed a small table between the chairs, gave them a glass each, and laid out Mallorcan white wine and a pitcher of water. "You don't have to stay, Luisa." Therese Mende smiled at the woman. "My talk with Herr Lubisch will probably go on for a while, don't worry."

Luisa glanced critically at Robert Lubisch and then left.

There were low, shaded lamps mounted on the wall on the left- and right-hand sides of the terrace, and their soft, yellowish light illuminated the tiled floor. They did not sit down until the front door had been locked shut. Therese Mende said calmly, as if talking to herself, "Frau Albers called me just before her death. She had found out that I was married to Wilhelm Peters and that I had been suspected of murder back then." She looked at him. "You know about this?"

Robert nodded. She went on, her voice cracking from time to time. "You say you came across the story, so I can probably assume it was you who gave her the photo?" Again, he nodded mutely. Therese Mende smiled bitterly. "I always knew my past would catch up with me eventually. A worry that has accompanied my life ever since I left, all those years ago. A kind of certainty, almost, that it would happen someday." She shivered and pulled the shawl tighter around her shoulders. Then she went on, her voice firm. "I told Frau Albers I would let my lawyers loose on her if she dared to spread half-truths. But she was a journalist, and it was clear to me that she wouldn't let go." She cleared her throat. "But please, tell me about yourself first."

Robert told the story of his father, his death and his papers, the photograph, and how he had come across Rita Albers. "You see," he said in conclusion, "the police seem to think I had something to do with Frau Albers's death. I didn't, or at least I didn't kill her. But if her death did in fact have something to do with that photo, then I feel guilty."

Therese Mende smiled out at the sea. She said, quite neutrally, "And now you want to know if I had something to do with it."

Robert Lubisch said nothing for a moment, then asked, "Does that really surprise you?"

She looked at him. Her face was tanned, and the pale fine lines around her blue eyes stood out in contrast. "No, it's probably not surprising. I've been suspected of murder once before."

"Do you know how my father came to have the photo? I mean, did you know him?"

There was a short pause.

She did not answer. Instead, she asked, "Have you allowed some time for this?"

He told her he would be leaving on Sunday. He felt a slight unease, suspecting he had relinquished control.

Therese Mende talked, telling him about her youth in the lower Rhine, her parents and friends, and the war. Sometimes she broke off for minutes at a time, looking out to sea as if fishing for the right words there. And when she talked about the prisoner of war named Yuri, he thought he saw again the expression that had so moved him in the photograph. She told him about her love for Yuri and his escape.

It was long after midnight when she closed her eyes, exhausted, and said, "I'm tired. Come again tomorrow morning. Let's say about ten."

The wine and the water were finished, and together they carried the pitcher, the bottle, and the glasses into the kitchen. Robert thanked her for the frankness of her account.

"Over the years, I thought I had distanced myself from it all," she said quietly. "When I went away, in 1950, I only wanted one thing: to forget. Start a new life. But you don't forget. You cut those years off, and what's left is a kind of inexplicable grief that overcomes you every now and then."

Chapter 33

April 24, 1998

He said something to Lili, but she turned her head away, offended because he had ignored her unambiguous nudging at the feeding bowl when he came in. He took an hourglass from the shelf and sat down at the kitchen counter. He owned at least fifty hourglasses; the particularly fine and expensive ones lived in a glass case in the living room. The cases were made of cherrywood, silver, and brass, decorated with figures or painted with great skill. He had bought a gold one in England: it measured out three minutes and was offered as a timer for tea.

This one was made of marble. It was four inches high and measured out fifteen minutes. He loved this visible, silent way of passing the time. Marlene crept up on him, placed her forepaws against his thigh, and looked at him intently with her green eyes. He scratched her head. "Maybe the guys in Homicide are right and it was something to do with a relationship. Maybe I'm getting ahead of myself." Marlene curled up in his lap. "This Gerhard. When Therese Peters disappears, he looks around halfheartedly for a bit and then closes the file. It was convenient for him that she disappeared—I'm sure of it." Marlene meowed, and he stroked her marmalade fur. "You're a clever girl."

Lili turned her head, looked at Karl reproachfully, and closed her eyes in boredom, as if to say, Creep!

Karl did not allow himself to be distracted. "And Paul says Gerhard has skeletons in his closet."

He pushed Marlene onto the bench beside him and stood up. He opened a can of cat food in the pantry. Lili and Marlene leapt to the floor and paced frantically to and fro in front of the feeding bowls. "If this Wilhelm was killed back then, and if his wife did it, where did she put him? They dug up the plot of land. Says so in the police report. But the cottage is isolated, fields and meadows all around." He filled the two bowls with food. When he looked up, half the fine-grained time already lay in the lower glass cylinder.

He had found the timer in an antiques shop in Nimwegen, and the owner had said, when he turned it over again after fifteen minutes, "So, now time runs back again." The hourglass was nothing special, and perhaps he had only bought it because he liked this remark so much.

As he was returning it to the shelf, he remembered. "Friday. Today's Friday, isn't it," he said, adding a reproachful, "Why didn't you say anything?" directed at the cats.

He picked up his jacket and left the house in a hurry. If he was lucky, he would find Paul at the Linden Tree pub. And without Hanna.

The pub was full of customers. The regulars were playing skat at the big old oak table, the bar was packed solid, and a couple of youths were playing billiards in the small adjoining room. A wide brass shade hung over the regulars' table, and dense cigar smoke curled in its light. Some of the shelves behind the bar were glassed in, protecting trophies and medals from the local marksmen's association, decorated with pennants and ribbons.

Paul was sitting by himself, as he always did, at the small table next to the counter. He sometimes joined in the general conversation, but usually he just listened to the others, drank two or three beers, and drove home. Karl rapped his knuckles on the bar, said, "Evening, all," and ordered a dark ale.

Lothar, the owner, immediately started questioning him about the murder, though he did not use the word, referring instead to "the woman who died over there." Karl was reminded of the saying, "He who lives by the sword will die by the sword," and thought Lothar had chosen an interesting turn of phrase.

"So tell me, have you caught anyone yet? Was it someone from around here?"

"All in good time," Karl replied evasively, looking over at Paul. Schwers, the painter and decorator, joined in. "Was it a robbery or what?" Karl shrugged. "Maybe. I'm not in charge of the investigation."

There was a roar from the youths at the billiards table, and Sebastian came over to the bar. "Six vodkas on Marius's tab," he said, grinning broadly. When he saw Karl, he said hello and left hurriedly.

Sebastian had always been in trouble. At fourteen he had broken into his own school; he had been caught selling suspect cell phones, and, most recently, he had stolen a car. Karl caught himself thinking, *What if it really was a robbery that went wrong?*

He watched Sebastian, skillfully placing the six shot glasses between his long fingers and avoiding eye contact with him. No. No, the boy would have run away. He would never have struck the woman from behind.

He took his ale and sat down at the table opposite Paul. He came to the point immediately.

"I went to see Theo Gerhard."

Paul did not look up; his eyes dived deeper into his glass of beer.

"He told me Therese Peters was a slut, whereas he was a thoroughly upstanding citizen who had always done his duty. And no problems during the war. Everything by the book, he says, otherwise he would never have been able to get back into the police force."

Paul looked up at Karl calmly. "Is that what he says? Must be true then."

"For goodness' sake, Paul, if you know something . . . I mean, tell me truthfully, do you think Gerhard had something to do with Albers's death?"

"I don't know." He looked past Karl at the regulars' table. "He could have." He took a sip of beer. "That table over there," he said, "it's pretty old—did you know that? Four years ago Lothar had a one-hundredth-anniversary party, and the table is probably as old as that . . . They've always sat there, all of them. When I was eight or nine, my father used to bring me in here occasionally. Gerhard and Peters sat there, and Hollmann, and the rest of them in their fancy uniforms. It made an impression on me. The flashes on their shoulders, the shiny buttons, the pistols at their belts."

Karl said nothing. Hermann Gärtner banged the table and laid down his cards. "The rest are mine," he said triumphantly in his high, feminine voice.

"We had two prisoners of war at the farm, and Peters used to come and check on them regularly. He seemed to respect my father, or at least he let quite a few things pass. The Russians ate with us, and in winter my father used to let them sleep in the house. Peters knew about it, but he never reported us." He snorted with laughter briefly. "It wasn't until long after the war that I found out his Aryan credentials weren't all that clean. His mother, Erna, came from one of the neighboring farms. The farmer was her father, and he acknowledged her as his daughter, but her mother, that's to say Wilhelm's grandma, was one of the maids, and her background certainly wasn't Aryan. They got Wilhelm his Aryan certificate by registering her as the farmer's legitimate daughter by his wife. When Peters and Gerhard beat up one of the Russians, my father went to see Wilhelm in the town hall and said to him, 'If you want to go on being an Aryan, I'd advise you never to lay a finger on any of my workers again.'"

He fell silent, holding his glass by the stem and twiddling it back and forth. He shook his head in resignation.

"When I came out of school, Peters would often pull up in that big car of his and give me a ride. 'Hey, Paul,' he'd say, 'I'm going over to your place. Do you want to come?' and the other boys would envy me. I was as proud as could be."

He raised his glass, looked over at Lothar, and nodded.

"The Russians were taken away in the fall of 1943. I had no idea why, and when I asked at home, all I got from Hanna and my father was, 'That needn't concern a snot-nosed kid like you.' I didn't know Therese had been arrested too. I hadn't seen her for a few days, and when I asked Hanna, she told me she'd gone away.

"Then Peters started giving me rides again, even though he didn't need to go to our place. He asked me if I'd seen one of the Russians with Therese, told me it was my patriotic duty to tell him everything. Therese had gotten involved with the enemy and had betrayed her people and the fatherland, he said. People like her were a threat to our final victory, and I would be doing Germany a great service if I had seen anything."

Lothar brought a beer and made a mark on the beer mat. Karl ordered another dark ale. Paul leaned forward, pushed his glass to one side, picked up the beer mat, and turned it over and over in his hand.

"I told him I'd seen them together at the edge of the forest from time to time, and that they had hugged and kissed each other." He snapped the beer mat in two and looked at Karl. "He praised me, said this was an important and secret matter, and that I shouldn't discuss it with anyone." He looked down and nodded to himself. "And I thought

I was a hero. Me, little Paul. I was sharing a secret of the utmost national importance with SS Squad Leader Peters."

Lothar brought the dark ale and looked reproachfully at Paul's hands, which were busy tearing the beer mat into smaller and smaller pieces. "Hey, what are you doing? How am I supposed to know what to charge you if you tear up the beer mat?"

"Three," said Paul, looking up at Lothar.

"I know," Lothar growled back, making three marks on a new beer mat and pushing it up to the far end of the table, out of Paul's reach.

Lothar had been back behind the bar for several minutes, but Paul had fallen silent.

"What happened to Therese?" asked Karl cautiously.

"She was released after a few days. Gerhard had beaten her half to death during questioning." He pushed away the scraps of beer mat. "She never said. She never said she knew about my telling on her."

It took Karl a moment. "I don't understand. She knew, and she married him anyway?"

Paul shook his head.

"She knew I betrayed her. But she thought I had told Gerhard. She didn't know about Wilhelm's part in the story until much later."

Karl was not given to agitation, but right now he was feeling slightly nervous. "So did she really do it? Did she kill Wilhelm Peters back then?"

Paul fished for the beer mat at the end of the table and waved to Lothar. He paid, and Karl hurriedly put some money on the table too.

Karl was on foot. He walked Paul to his old Mercedes.

He made one more attempt: "Did she do it?"

Paul unlocked the car. He shook his head slowly, and Karl did not know whether he was answering his question or refusing to answer.

Chapter 34

April 25, 1998

Despite taking a sleeping pill, Therese Mende had had a restless night. It was not until the early hours of the morning that she dropped off, her sleep foggy, peopled with the old shadows circling round and round. Fragmented images lining up disconnectedly and declaring her guilty.

When she woke up in the morning, she could not get the words *Keep silent* out of her head, and in the bathroom, in front of the mirror, she applied it for the first time not to her past but to herself. "I'll keep silent till the day I die," she whispered at her reflection, and the words struck her with such force that she staggered.

Tillmann had known her story; maybe his death had been so distressing, and had left such a void in its wake, precisely because she had gone back to bearing the weight of her guilt alone afterward.

A stabbing pain in her chest extended into her left arm, taking her breath away. The thought that her daughter might, like Robert Lubisch, go unsuspectingly hunting about after her death and find out that her mother had lied to her for her whole life was suddenly unbearable. And what would she find? The remnants of a time that had become foul and rotten over the years, handed down by people who had convinced themselves they were blameless.

She took a heart pill. After breakfast she felt stronger again.

Robert too had had a short night, but he arrived on time. Therese invited him to join her on her daily walk.

They went down the narrow street, and she asked about his life in Hamburg. He spoke freely, telling her about his wife, Maren, his work in the hospital, and also about his father and his struggles with him when he decided against following him into the business and became a doctor. "I now think he was always a stranger to me. As a child, I sought out his company, his affection. I wanted him to like me. Later, my efforts went in the opposite direction—probably because they had been so fruitless—and now that I really think about it, I didn't have his attention until I started to rebel."

The first swimmers of the day were gathering on the beach, spreading out their towels and picnic blankets, inflating orange armbands on children's thin arms, dipping their toes in the water, and flinching away with a shiver.

Once they had left the bay behind, Therese abruptly resumed her story from the night before.

1943/44

The days went by and there was no news from Yuri. Wilhelm came to visit, but he was wary and did not mention her promise to marry him. She avoided talking about Yuri and did not tell him she had seen him one more time, but when there was still no news after two weeks, she could bear it no longer.

They were walking side by side through the town. It was mid-November.

"I'm afraid. They're bound to be looking for him. If they had caught him, you'd know, wouldn't you?" She had thrust her hands deep into her coat pockets. He was pushing her bicycle with one hand and had his arm around her shoulders.

"They haven't caught him, because no one's looking for him," he said. He continued matter-of-factly. "The official report says Yuri made a break for it, and Gerhard stood him up against the van and shot him." He stopped and looked at her. "He didn't shoot him, of course. The dead man was someone else." Therese clenched her fists in her pockets. She looked down at the ground, not daring to look at him, and heard Yuri saying, as if from far off, "There was another prisoner in the van."

Therese Mende and Robert Lubisch sat on a bench that served as both resting place and viewpoint at a widening of the path. She said, "Look, that's how it is with the truth. I could say I just wanted to save Yuri's life, and it's the truth. I could say the other one would have been shot anyway, and that's probably a truth too. But it's also true that my request for Yuri's life extinguished another life."

Robert Lubisch leaned forward and rested his elbows on his knees. They looked out to sea. Therese's words came softly, mingling with the rhythm of the waves as she went on with her story.

They never touched on the subject again, and life went on so unquestioningly that sometimes she could scarcely bear it. She waited for news from Yuri, thinking he was probably in Holland, but the only mail came from the private in France. At the end of 1943, she wrote to him one last time. She thanked him for his trouble, and explained that circumstances had changed and he should no longer write to her.

Alwine's father had fallen on the Eastern Front during the days Therese spent in jail, and Alwine's grief was boundless. It was Frau Kalder who received Therese's delayed condolence visit, and she apologized on behalf of her daughter. Alwine withdrew entirely: not only did she avoid contact with Therese, but she also stopped speaking to Wilhelm. Shortly before Christmas—by now, the last of the livestock had been requisitioned from the farms and the Kalder estate—they met by chance in the street. Alwine was almost unrecognizable. She had lost a lot of weight, her eyes were dull, and her finely shaped mouth, in Therese's memory always laughing, was pinched with bitterness. They stood facing each other, like strangers. Alwine said, as if to herself, "We're moving in with relatives in southern Germany after Christmas. A manager's being put in here until the war's over." Abruptly, she said, "So you're going to marry him?" Therese lowered her head, ashamed. She told her, her words at first halting and uncertain, then in a torrent sprinkled with constant apologies, what had happened after her arrest. Alwine interrupted her before she had finished. "You're lying, Therese," she hissed. "Why are you lying to me? Gerhard told me, well before you were arrested, that the two of you were getting married." She turned and left. Therese stood motionless in the cold for a long time. When at last she moved, her limbs were stiff, and she staggered home on unsteady legs. The suspicion that whispered in her head at first, then grew louder and louder, seemed monstrous.

Wilhelm had invited her out to a pub in Kleve the following evening. She did not want to talk to him about it until they were there, but she could not hold it back. While they were still in the car, she asked, "Why did Theo tell Alwine we were getting married before I was even arrested?" Wilhelm reacted immediately, with an easy laugh.

"Oh, Theo! He can't understand why I don't give in to Alwine. Why I don't propose to her." He pulled over on the right-hand side of the road, stopped the car, and looked at Therese. He caressed her face. "I told him there was only one woman I would marry, and that was you." He sighed. "Theo's a clumsy oaf. He told Alwine."

How relieved she was. Suddenly, her suspicions seemed absurd. "It's worrying about Yuri," she told herself. "Worrying about Yuri is driving me mad."

Robert Lubisch and Therese Mende went on walking. They reached a place where the cliff path narrowed and led down to the next bay. They had to walk in single file. The sun stood high and white in the sky, and a gentle, salty breeze wafted in from the sea, bringing with it a pleasant coolness. There was a pine forest immediately behind the small beach. There were no hotels or holiday complexes here, just a rudimentary wooden hut for a beach bar and a handful of swimmers.

Therese turned to Robert Lubisch. "They make excellent coffee," she said with a smile, and headed straight for a table under a straw-covered sunshade. The young man behind the bar greeted her with a wave and, without being asked, brought two double espressos and a jug of water.

The fragrance of the pines mingled with the salty smell of the sea. It was pleasantly still, and Robert seemed to feel time passing more slowly here, more deliberately. He looked straight at Therese and asked her the question that had been preoccupying him since the previous evening. "The private," he began cautiously, "the private who wrote to you from France was called Friedhelm Lubisch, wasn't he?"

She avoided his gaze, but nodded in confirmation. The next question made his spine tingle, but it seemed quite natural. "Did he visit you? Did my father come to Kranenburg after the war?"

Therese Mende stirred her coffee. "Let me tell you the story in order," she said deliberately, and patted his hand reassuringly.

By early 1944, only the fanatics still believed in the "Final Victory." There were whispers of a wonder weapon everywhere. A wonder weapon that would turn the tide. At the same time, news of fallen husbands, sons, and brothers reached homes every day. Death became normal. Those months were insubstantial in her memory. She hurried ahead from one day to the next, closing her eyes and ears, and raced home on her bicycle in the evening, ruled by one thought alone: Today! Today there would be news of Yuri.

Her day-to-day work in the factory, her encounters with Wilhelm, taking care of the house and garden—these were just actions and words that followed, one upon the other, because they had to. They belonged to a realm of shadows lurking quietly beneath her hope for a sign of life from Yuri.

But hope dissipated, dropping soundlessly away at the margins of those deadened days. First it happened during the nights, when she counted on her fingers the weeks that had passed, then on Sundays in church, when she asked God's forgiveness for having bought Yuri's life with that of another man, and finally in broad daylight, when she woke up from her trance in shock and knew with sudden certainty that she would have received news long since if he had been alive.

"The worst thing," she whispered into her coffee cup, "was that my memory of him faded. His features, his body, his smile, the way he walked. It all melted away, like snow on the first warm days after the winter. Only his voice is left to me. The way he rolled the *r* in my name: I can still hear it today."

By the summer, the last few halfway battle-fit men had been conscripted too, the red swastika banners hung faded and tired in front of the town hall, and the Western Front was coming relentlessly closer. She proceeded through the days, her feet heavy and dragging, and when the factory sirens wailed and they all ran into the basements, she would stand up quite slowly, walk casually along the empty hallways, and think, *Now. Now, at last.*

By August the front was at Eindhoven, and at night there was a red glow on the horizon. The rumbling of artillery was a distant thunderstorm beneath a starlit sky. Her father did not come home anymore; he lived at the military hospital, and her mother, it seemed to her, at the church.

Wilhelm was organizing the home front. One Friday he said to her, "Therese, please let's get married. You promised, and I've given you nearly a year. I don't want to wait any longer."

And she had nodded. She had nodded because he had done everything to save Yuri's life. She had nodded because she owed it to him. She had nodded because a life after the war was unthinkable.

Therese pushed her cup into the center of the table. "We got married on August 25, 1944, in the town hall. Not a big ceremony. My mother and Wilhelm's parents were there. Martha and an employee from the administration were our witnesses."

She fell silent for a long time. Then she ran her hand over the tabletop, as if to erase the picture, and stood up. Robert stood up too, and went over to the bar to pay for their drinks. Therese held him back. "No, no. I have a cup of coffee here every day, and I pay at the end of the month."

As they set off on their way back, he asked, "And your father wasn't there?"

She shook her head. "No. I went to Bedburg-Hau and asked after him, but all they could tell me was that he was in one of the many temporary hospitals that had been set up: schools, pub function rooms, public buildings. I didn't find him." She paused briefly. "I don't think I even wanted to find him."

Chapter 35

April 25, 1998

The station was officially not staffed on Saturdays, but Karl van den Boom was on-site at nine o'clock nevertheless. If something within his sphere of responsibility happened at night or on a weekend, the calls were automatically transferred to headquarters in Kleve. He called there to ask. A female colleague told him that eight-year-old Moritz Geerkes had been reported missing late in the evening, but he had been picked up in a park three hours later, with a friend. And a car had been reported stolen. "Otherwise, all quiet your way," she said, and hung up.

Then he called Kalkar and reached Manfred Steiner. "Hard work," Steiner said. "The ex-husband can be eliminated—he has a watertight alibi." Karl could hear him hammering away at his keyboard. Steiner paused and said, "Forensics found some fingerprints on the desk that we can't identify. For comparison purposes, we need prints from the two gardeners who found the body. If you're in the office anyway, can you take care of that?" Karl thought for a moment, then agreed.

He called Schoofs, the landscape-gardening company. Both men were there.

"What do you want from them?" asked Matthias Schoofs.

"Fingerprints," Karl replied. "We found some, and now we need to know whether they belong to your employees or perhaps to the perpetrator."

"I see. In that case, all right." Schoofs promised to send his men over within the hour.

Over a cup of coffee and a cheese sandwich, Karl thought about his evening with Paul. He had always been an odd character. Karl had been born here, and even when he was a child, the Hövers were surrounded by this aura of being out of the ordinary. He could still see old man Höver in his mind's eye. He had died in the early sixties, and Karl remembered him as an imposing figure well into his old age. The farm had been partly destroyed during the war; the two eldest sons had had to join up right at the beginning and had been killed. The agricultural side had never really recovered, even though the father, Paul, and Hanna were all hardworking. They lived a life apart: they were seen only on Sundays, at church, and after the old man died, Hanna moved to Kleve and became a nurse. Paul inherited the farm and married Sofia. She was not a farmer. After two miscarriages, she was unlikely to have any children, and she was never really healthy. Paul leased out and sold off more and more of the arable and pasture land because he could not cope with it all on his own. "Managed downward," people used to say when they talked about the Höver farm in those days. At least, that was the gossip and barroom chatter that Karl had heard all these years.

During the seventies and eighties, a lot of people had shown interest in the cottage. It had a lovely position, and the house, with skilled work, could be renovated. People from the Ruhr had come and, so it was said at the time, offered good money. But Paul had not sold. When Rita Albers turned up, he was probably up to his ears in debt, and he agreed to the lease.

Karl positioned himself by the window of the guardroom and looked out at the parking lot. The linden tree that kept the office pleasantly cool in summer was showing its first new shoots, and within a few days they would be lending a greenish-yellow hue to the light of the room. When that happened, he was particularly fond of installing himself here, sitting by the door whenever he could. A swift had just flown by, with its high-pitched *srii, srii* call, when a car marked "Schoofs Landscape Gardening" parked under the linden.

Klaus Breyer and Jan Neumann, wearing their green overalls, strolled in.

While Breyer's fingerprints were being taken, Jan grumbled to himself, wanting to know whether the prints were stored and might end up in some card index somewhere. Van den Boom reassured him. He pressed Breyer's fingers onto an ink pad and then paper, and asked, "Why were you there, in fact? I mean, what was the job?"

Jan exploded again. "See?" he said to Klaus Breyer. "I told you. If they don't find the guy who did this, they'll pin it on us instead. That's the way they work."

Van den Boom shook his head. "Calm down, son. Nobody suspects you. I just want to know whether you were supposed to be planting flowers or cutting down trees or mowing the lawn." Breyer wiped his fingers with a tissue. "It was about the well. We were supposed to install a new well."

Van den Boom waved Jan over. He was hesitant at best about offering his fingers.

When the two men had gone, Karl decided to take the prints to Steiner himself. He could have another think in peace on the way. Something the gardeners had said was going round and round in his head, and he wanted to discuss it with Steiner.

Chapter 36

April 25, 1998

Therese invited Robert in for a bite to eat, and they sat down on the covered part of the terrace. Luisa served sherry first; ten minutes later, she brought roasted mushrooms and peppers, Manchego cheese with red onions, olives, Serrano ham, and a baguette. They ate in silence for a while, and Robert enjoyed the taste, the appearance, and the fine aroma of the food. Therese seemed lost in thought, and he had already learned that he must not push her, that she would go on with her story when she was ready.

He took another piece of Manchego, and she took up the thread.

1944

Hell began in September. German troops were fleeing in confusion across the Dutch border. Anyone who could handle a spade or shovel was ordered to report to the playing field. They were transported to the border in trucks to dig antitank defenses. Therese worked side by side with Hanna and her father-in-law, Peters, the pharmacist.

Sunday, September 17, was the Feast of the Cross. Mass was to be said in the morning, with the procession to take place in the afternoon. Therese and her mother were on their way to church with the Hövers, when fighter bombers came flying low over the plain, firing machine guns and tossing out hand grenades. Whenever the sound of the engines came close, they would throw themselves into the ditches at the edge of the fields. The dirt around them would spray up, then fall back to earth like black rain, and as the staccato sound of the machine-gun bursts moved away again, she would feel a moment of astonishment. A floating deafness. It was not until the others started moving, crawling out of the ditch, that she understood she was still alive.

A little before they reached Kranenburg, several bullets struck her mother. No tears. An immobility in her mind, blocked by a single *no*. Always just *no*. Never known another word. An instinctive mobility in her limbs, which followed never-conceived laws. With Höver's help, she carried her mother as far as the church wall and stopped there, sitting with her mother's head resting in her lap. She rocked her upper body to and fro, saw all that blood on her clothes, thought it was her own, heard the singing in the church: "Holy God, we praise thy name."

Höver came back with two neighbors. "Give her to us," he said, and they took her mother from her. She watched, motionless, as they carried her to the cemetery chapel. Sheltering behind the church wall, she watched the men throw themselves and the body to the ground as fresh rounds of machine-gun fire came rattling out of the sky and struck the wall. She saw Höver's face over her, lifting her up, and it seemed obvious that they were going to carry her to the chapel and lay her down beside her mother. But he took her into the church with him and sat her down on the pew, between him and Hanna. Hanna was crying, and it was not until the service was over that she felt an increasingly powerful trembling come over her, beyond control, and it finally shook her out of her daze. They buried her mother the next day, hurriedly, along with four other casualties. No funeral shroud, no coffin with a pillow and a beautiful cover. A rough wooden box, a short prayer, a hurried blessing.

The days that followed were nights. The skies black with the smoke of burning villages, farms, forests, avenues of trees. The whole country seemed to be in flames, blazing red and roaring with pain. Wounded and dying soldiers in the houses, animals perishing in fields and roads, the land torn up, bombed beyond recognition, and the people deaf from the noise of machine guns, bombs, shells, and aircraft. In October, Kranenburg was officially evacuated. Therese went to Bedburg-Hau, along with the Hövers. A horse cart, drawn by the last ox, carried the Hövers' scant remaining possessions along the road. Therese had only a suitcase. She and Hanna were assigned to care for the wounded. There were no medicines and no painkillers. In truth, they were there only to hold the hands of dying men. A few days later, she saw her father again for the first time, and at first she did not recognize him. He was a shadow of his former self; his eyeglasses were held together with tape, and one lens was broken. When she told him about her mother's death, he nodded mutely. No questions. The next day too, when she told him she had married Wilhelm, he reacted in the same way, nodding and stroking her cheek absently. His fatigue was eating him up from the inside, like a flame beneath a glass bulb consuming the last of the oxygen.

Luisa came to clear the table, and Therese asked for two coffees. She leaned back in her chair and ran her hand over the massive tabletop. "It wasn't until the war was over and we went to see Mother's grave that he cried and asked how it happened. There was no time for mourning in the winter of 1944/45, and sometimes I think that was one of the tragedies of that war, perhaps of every war. When we don't have time to mourn, we lose a dimension of our humanity."

Luisa brought coffee in two delicate white porcelain cups and placed a matching sugar bowl on the table. Robert stirred a spoonful of sugar into his. A small dog yapped excitedly on the property next door.

The Hövers and Therese did not return to the cottage until May, and they took with them Wilhelm's parents, whose house had burned down along with the pharmacy. Peace. There was peace at last, but the word was still fragile. At first, as they traveled through the shattered towns, passing bomb craters and the black ruins of trees along the road, she could not work out why the voices of other people, their footsteps, and the creaking wheels of handcarts seemed to be the only sounds. Not until the next day, when she was alone for a moment, did she understand. An infinite silence. The spring sky high and blue, and not a bird to be seen for miles. She could not even hear the cawing of the usually omnipresent rooks, and she realized she was still listening for the sound of approaching aircraft. For years she continued to listen like that, seeking, though the birds had long since returned, the distant rumbling of engines beneath their song.

The Höver farmhouse was badly damaged, and the barn had burned down. The six of them moved into the cottage, and, every morning, they would go over to the house first thing to clear rubble and break rocks. After four weeks, Hanna, Paul, and old Höver moved back into the part of the house that was now more or less habitable.

They had news of Wilhelm late that summer. He was a British prisoner. Frau Peters and her husband lay in each other's arms, weeping with joy. Therese too was glad that Wilhelm was alive. He wrote: *I was burned on my arms and legs in the battle of the Reichswald, but I'm now on the way to recovery.* And on the back of the sheet of coarse gray paper he complained: *Many soldiers have already been released, but we from the SS are interrogated again and again. They call us war criminals, and we have to prove where we served during the war. They don't understand that we were all just doing our duty.*

The Hövers were allotted four half-starved cows. Therese replanted the vegetable garden, and when her father came back, she took care of him. He seemed to be dwindling away before her eyes, as if a monstrous effort of strength was now at last taking its toll. It was not until a few days before he died, in 1946, that he asked her why she had married Wilhelm. She told him. He stroked her cheek with his hand, now bony and lined with blue veins, and nodded. His touch was of such tenderness, his eyes so full of understanding, that she perceived it as a kind of absolution. Three days later, he lay dead in his bed, and painful as the loss was, she also felt gratitude when she saw the peace in his features.

They buried him beside her mother. More than a hundred people came to the funeral to offer their condolences. They included all those who had avoided her and her parents in the years just past. They did it as a matter of course. Therese, who hesitated in front of the first hands held out to her, thought herself petty; these people had all made a new beginning, and only she had not.

The sun had migrated across the bay, and the tall palm trees that stood on the boundary of the neighboring property cast their shadows over the uncovered part of the terrace. In this new light, the blooms of the hibiscus bushes in their large clay pots changed from reddish orange to bloodred. Therese Mende stood up. "Come. Let's sit down in front, by the water. The sun has lost its heat, and the breeze will feel good." They stood at the balustrade and looked out over the sea. Swimmers' voices floated on the wind, and Robert occasionally thought he caught a name being called out. "When you think how millions of people died appalling deaths at that time, my story seems a bit foolish. But pain doesn't stop just because you know others have to bear much greater pain." She fell silent for a moment and ran her left hand through her hair, as if she wanted to wipe the thought away.

Back then, she shook all those hands, listened to their words of sympathy, saw them avoiding her gaze, ashamed, and she thought for the first time that she could not stay. It was as if all her losses were piled up here, among all these people. Her mother, Leonard, Jacob, Yuri, and her father. Even Frau Hoffmann, who had been selling groceries in her shop since the end of the war, demanding extortionate prices from those without a ration card, offered her condolences. She did not show a second of embarrassment. Quite matter-of-factly, she said, "I'm so sorry, child. He was a wonderful man. His death is a loss for us all, but in these difficult times you have to look ahead." And then, after the burial, Theo Gerhard was waiting for her in front of the cemetery. He was wearing an armband that indicated he was a police officer, and she could not believe her eyes. He said he had to do it, back then, that he had orders as to how—and he actually said it—enemy whores were to be treated. When she said nothing, he became uneasy. "You shouldn't forget that I saved that Russian's life," he said quietly, and then he shuffled off swiftly.

Therese Mende pushed a strand of hair away from her face and looked at Robert Lubisch. "Wilhelm's parents stayed another full year, and then they moved in with relatives in Schwerte. In the spring of 1948, Wilhelm came back, released from captivity. He had a document that described him as a follower, and he showed it to everyone. In some absurd way he was proud of it. Three months later, he got a job in the planning department, provisionally equipped as it was. Our marriage wasn't happy. He loved me, he was considerate and hardworking, but I couldn't return his feelings. He felt it. And then came the summer of 1950. For the first time since the end of the war, the Marksmen's Club held its annual fair."

Chapter 37

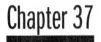

April 25, 1998

When Karl arrived at headquarters, there were only four cars in the parking lot, and a Saturday-like silence reigned in the hallways of the building. He laid the envelope with the fingerprints on Steiner's desk.

"I thought I'd come myself and ask whether there was anything new."

Steiner smiled with satisfaction. "And how," he said amiably. "We know who Therese Peters is."

"Hmm," said Karl, waiting. Several seconds passed, and then he said, "And? Who is she?"

Steiner looked at him. "Therese Mende. She's worth millions, and she lives in Mallorca."

Karl whistled through his teeth. Then he asked, with a lightly ironic undertone, "And? Was she here, and did she kill Albers?"

Steiner grabbed his glasses, which were dangling in front of his chest. "So far we have no indications that she was here, but . . . someone like her wouldn't do it herself."

"Have you spoken to her?"

"No. Köbler, that journalist, left only a quarter of an hour ago. But it gets even better. Our colleagues in Hamburg report that Robert Lubisch has left the country, and guess where he is?" Steiner left a dramatic pause and then said, triumphantly, "He flew to Mallorca yesterday."

Karl sat down and rubbed his cheek and mouth with his left hand. "That means *he's* found her too."

Steiner snapped his glasses back and forth. "That's one possibility. The other would be that they knew each other already."

Karl shook his head slowly. "Come on, why would he have asked Albers to do any research if he already knew, and had known for a long time, who Therese Peters is today?"

Steiner sighed. "That's true enough, but we only know from him that he asked Albers to do the research. There's no other proof of it." He tapped the file lying open on his desk. "Neither the woman in the residents' registration office nor this Schröder from the archives mention her saying anything about a contract. What if Albers didn't have the photo from him, but ran across Lubisch in the course of her research and made contact with him? What if he wasn't happy about it?"

"Hmm." Karl ran it through in his mind. It was true, of course, that they did not know much about Robert Lubisch. "But if your investigations are tending in that direction, you must be assuming it has something to do with the disappearance of Wilhelm Peters, no?"

Steiner put his glasses on. "Yes, that seems probable. In any case, we don't have anything else at the moment, and Köbler says Albers was talking about a pretty big story. She didn't have everything put together yet, but she had obviously stumbled upon a hornets' nest and somebody stopped her."

Karl seemed absorbed in staring at the stack of files on Steiner's desk. "The gardeners had a contract to dig a new well," he said pensively, without looking up.

Steiner frowned. He shook his head uncomprehendingly. "So what?"

"I'm just saying. I don't rightly know how you dig a well these days, but they would certainly have had to drill or dig a hole on the property. The report says the land was searched back then, but Gerhard was in charge, and he . . . well, he has skeletons in his closet."

Steiner said nothing for a moment. "You think . . ."

Karl stood up. "Exactly. I think. I'll have a word with Schoofs. It would be interesting to know who knew about the new well."

At the garden center, Matthias Schoofs and his wife were busy moving young plants into the greenhouse. Schoofs raised his hand in greeting. "What's up now, Karl?" he called out, without interrupting his work. "The boys have finished for the day. They won't be back till Monday." He paused. "Don't you ever take the weekend off?"

Karl laughed good-naturedly. "I do, I do. I just have one more question about that well at the Albers place."

Schoofs gestured dismissively. "We never did it. The problem had taken care of itself."

"Yes, yes. What I'm interested in . . . I mean, who knew about it? Who knew you were going to dig a well there?"

Schoofs shrugged. "How should I know who she told? Here it was only me, my wife, Jan, and Klaus who knew about it. Nobody else." He went over to a metal rack holding wooden crates of lettuce plants, snapped the brake lever up with the back of his foot, and pushed the rack toward the greenhouse. Karl was disappointed.

"Oh, I called Hanna. Asked her if she remembered where the old well was, and how deep it was."

Karl went over to Schoofs and helped him push. He felt a catch in his throat as he asked, "And what did she say?"

"That it had been blocked up since the war. She couldn't remember how deep it was." Once in the greenhouse, Schoofs went round the rack and kicked the brake back on.

Karl thanked him and wished him a good weekend. He sat in his car for several minutes. Hanna and Paul. Everything in him resisted this suspicion; everything told him not to drive over to the Höver farm. He started his car and drove away only when he saw Schoofs looking worriedly down the driveway at him.

At the Höver farm, he found Hanna in the stables.

"Now what?" she said, by way of greeting, as she cleared the horse manure from a stall.

"I need a word with you," he said tonelessly. Hanna leaned on her pitchfork and looked at him calmly.

"About what? We're busy," she retorted in her brusque way, looking at him suspiciously. "Besides, Paul's out."

"It's about the well." Karl opened the half-height stable door and saw Hanna's face wince in distress. She tapped the pitchfork tines rhythmically against the concrete floor but said nothing. He leaned against a wooden post with a leather halter and bridle hanging on a hook. She laughed bitterly. "I'm sure you have time to let me finish here." She shoved the pitchfork into the straw and tossed it into the wheelbarrow, as if Karl were not present. And Karl knew she would not talk to him until she finished her work.

Chapter 38

April 25, 1998

Therese Mende pushed her chair back. "Wait here a moment, Robert. I'd like to get something and let Luisa know you're staying for dinner. I can tell her that, can't I?"

Robert Lubisch ran both hands through his hair. Then he said, "With pleasure." He brought his arms down, and now felt, just as he had when Rita Albers telephoned him, that anxiety, that shying away from what might yet come. Therese Mende disappeared into the house, and the sense of foreboding, a nameless weight on his shoulders, increased. He threw his head back and looked up at the high, soft blue of the sky. He had always searched for a stain on his father's snow-white waistcoat, had always wanted, while his father was still alive, to be able to mount a challenge to the self-control he had been so proud of. And now, he was quite sure of it; he was going to find it, and it would not just be a stain. He stood up and strode up and down the terrace; he had a momentary impulse to leave, to let things rest.

When Therese Mende came back, they sat down again, and she placed a leather wallet, a sort of envelope, on the table. She looked at him intently. "You can still leave." After a brief hesitation, he shook his head. "No," he said, suddenly decisive. "No, I can't do that. Not anymore."

She picked up the leather wallet and, as they spoke, held it tightly in her lap with both hands.

It was a hot day, that August 12, 1950, and it was the first Marksmen's Fair since the war. There was a carousel with a red-and-white-painted roof that shone in the sun. There was a stand selling raisin donuts, and the air was filled with the sticky-sweet smell of the sugar that people were licking off their fingers. The adults gathered around the drinks stand for beer, wine, and lemonade, and by the afternoon a good many had had too much to drink. Children lined up in front of a table to buy cotton candy. The motor that ran the centrifuge kept overheating. Whenever the vendor shouted, "No more for another half hour!" small hands would shove their tightly gripped five-pfennig coins back into the pockets of their shorts and skirts, and the children would go running off. A long counter had been set up in the main tent. A band played dance music. The whole community was there; people had come from the surrounding villages and farms, and groups of young people had come on their bicycles from as far away as Kleve. There were many strange faces. The heat mounted inside the tent, the smell of sweat mingled with cigarette and cigar smoke, and whenever Therese had had a dance and the band inserted a pause, she would go out to cool off a little. At about four, she sought refuge on the edge of the fairground, in the shadow of an oak tree, and watched the goings-on. She found Paul Höver behind the trunk. He had obviously drunk too much beer for his sixteen years and was throwing up.

She went up to him and said, "Oops, too much of a good thing, Paul?" Paul was visibly embarrassed, and asked her not to say anything to his father. He leaned against the trunk, slipped down, and sat there with his legs outstretched.

"Shall I take you home?" she asked cautiously, prepared for his pride not to allow it.

"No, no. It'll soon pass. I want to stay." He spoke slowly, but his words were clear.

Therese thought he would soon recover in the fresh air and sat down beside him. "I need a break myself."

Paul leaned his head against the trunk and looked at her with slightly troubled eyes. "Can I ask you something, Therese?"

She smiled. "But of course."

"Why did you marry Wilhelm, after what he did?"

She shook her head and asked, still smiling, "What do you mean?"

"That thing with Yuri back then. That's what I mean. With Yuri and you."

Suddenly, something ominous lay in the air. The cool of the shade, which had been pleasant, now felt cold. She folded her arms over her chest and rubbed her hands against her bare arms. "I don't understand what you mean," she said, and she could hear that her voice sounded rough and strange.

"Well, your being arrested, and because they shot Yuri anyway."

Therese Mende looked at Robert Lubisch. "I was relieved. Paul was just a child back then, and he'd obviously gotten everything wrong. I said, 'Oh, Paul, you were still little back then. You've gotten it all wrong.' But he shook his head."

Therese Mende looked down, staring at the leather wallet again.

Suddenly, Paul was in tears. "No, Therese, I haven't gotten it wrong. I was the one who betrayed you back then." He had buried his face in the crook of his arm.

She took hold of his thick hair and said, "Paul, I know you told Gerhard about me and Yuri. But you were a child. I'm not angry with you about that."

Paul calmed down gradually. He looked at her through tear-filled eyes. "You knew?"

She nodded. "Yes, but you're not to blame. Theo Gerhard's to blame."

Paul pulled his legs up and put his arms around them. He said, "But I told Wilhelm, not Gerhard."

In hindsight, it seemed to her that what he said reached only her ears at first, strange and false, his words distorted and unrecognizable. She knew too that she thought he was just drunk and falling to pieces.

She grabbed him by the shoulders and shook him. "That's not true, Paul. You told Gerhard, not Wilhelm." He started crying again. And then he said the words that snuffed out the light for her: "No, I told Wilhelm, and I saw him and Gerhard shoot Yuri in the clearing too."

She heard a shrill sound in her head, louder and louder, screaming, and behind it pictures falling one on top of the next, without rhyme or reason and yet, in sequence, seemingly logical. She heard Alwine saying, "You're going to marry him?" She saw Wilhelm at her bedside, swearing he knew nothing about it all. She heard Yuri asking, "What have you done, Therese? Why are they letting me go?" and saw him heading toward the forest in the fog. Forever.

Hope flared up in her for a moment. For a moment she thought Paul might have seen Gerhard shooting the stranger, and she said, "Wilhelm wasn't there. You saw Gerhard on the road, didn't you? It was Gerhard and a stranger," and her voice rose, breaking. But Paul shook his head and looked at her wide-eyed, as if it were only clear to him now what he had seen back then. As if he were only now realizing that she really had not known about all this. His voice came to her from afar. "No. You met Yuri behind the barn. I followed Yuri. Theo Gerhard and Wilhelm shot him in the clearing, from the lookout. That's the truth, Therese, I swear." Something tore, something fell, and Yuri disappeared into the fog and kept asking, endlessly, "What have you done? Why are they letting me go?"

The rest of the afternoon was deaf, mute, and blind. Days later, witnesses testified that she was screaming in front of the tent and attacked Wilhelm, and that Hanna had taken her home. But she did not remember. What she did remember was a sensation in her gut, as if she were swinging higher and higher, and it made her feel faint. She felt pressure in her head and then, as if the swing had reached its highest point, as if she had leaned her body back once too often and, at just the right moment, thrown her legs up at the sky, a feeling of floating.

Afterward, the pictures were not of her, or so she felt later. Her body sat in that flowery, blue summer dress, barefoot and motionless on the chair between the kitchen table and the cold stove.

She felt nothing. Empty of feeling.

She thought nothing. Empty of thought.

The door stood open. In the yard, the evening sucked the yellow out of the earth, tinting it darker and darker brown until the night extinguished all colors.

Hours must have gone by before she heard him. He was tipsy, singing and talking to himself. She picked up the poker that lay beside the range, positioned herself next to the entrance, and, when he reached the door, she struck.

He fell, and at the same time he was standing there.

He was lying on the floor, and at the same time he was breathing his boozy breath into her face at eye level.

He was lying on the floor, and at the same time he was reaching for the light switch.

He stood there, staring at the man lying on the floor, and suddenly seemed stone-cold sober. "You meant . . . me?" he asked, and his astonishment was genuine. He pointed at the man at his feet. The tip of the poker was embedded in his head. He said, "His name's Lubisch. He wanted to see you."

Therese Mende pressed the leather wallet to her chest and took a deep breath. Then she opened it and passed it across the table. "This is our wedding photo," she said neutrally, and Robert was looking at his father's young face. He did not dare to pick up the picture. His eyes went back and forth in disbelief between the photograph and Therese Mende. "I—I don't understand," he stammered.

"You see, Wilhelm understood the situation quickly, much more quickly than I did, and if it was true that I had quarreled with him at the fairground, then he knew Yuri's murder would come to light, that I wouldn't keep quiet. I learned from Hanna, later on, that Friedhelm Lubisch had been asking for me in the big tent. He wanted to come and visit me. Hanna told him I had left, but she could point out my husband to him. He spent the evening with Wilhelm, and probably told him his whole life story.

"That evening, as he knelt down beside Lubisch, Wilhelm seemed to understand immediately that this was his chance. He took the man's wallet with the discharge papers, ran into the bedroom, and packed a few things."

Robert put his hands in front of his face to fight off what he was hearing. And the suspicion that had been growing in the farthest reaches of his brain, ever since Therese Mende mentioned Wilhelm Peters's burns a few hours before, was now definitively confirmed. He could see his father's scarred upper arms and left calf in his mind's eye.

"A house fire, right at the beginning of the war," he had always claimed. His father!

It was dusk. An unreal, purple light lay over the water as Therese Mende stood up and returned with a bottle of cognac and two snifters. She poured generously. They drank in silence. Then she leaned forward. Her eyes were wet with tears. "When he left, he said, 'I can't help you anymore now. You have to take responsibility for this on your own. But you should know one thing: Everything I did then, I did for love.' He really said that. 'For love.'"

Chapter 39

April 25, 1998

Having spread fresh straw in the stall, Hanna brought the wheelbarrow into the barn, hung the pitchfork, point up, in a wooden rack in which more forks, rakes, shovels, and spades were tidily arranged in a row. Karl stood in the yard and watched her. He thought Hanna must be over seventy, but in her checked shirt and overalls, and with her industrious energy, she looked like a woman in her midfifties.

She came out of the barn and said, as she marched past him, in her abrupt way, "I'll get dressed. Then we can go."

Karl watched her walk toward the house. He thought he would clear up the death of Rita Albers now, and he felt neither pride nor satisfaction. He waited by his car. The Hövers' orchard and vegetable garden extended all the way to the road. A gentle breeze wafted through the fruit trees, which were in bloom. A brimstone butterfly settled on the roof of the car, apparently taking a short breather.

When she came out of the house, she had put on her good clothes, and it looked strange. She was wearing a white blouse with an elongated shawl collar, which she had tied in a large bow over her chest. The narrow gray skirt reached to her calves, and in her matching pumps she looked even taller than usual. Without a word, she went up to his car and got in on the passenger side.

Karl sat behind the wheel. She looked out of the window and said, "I've written Paul a note. I'm sure he'll follow." On the way to the police station, she sat quietly beside him. Her thoughts seemed to revolve entirely around her brother. At one point she said, "He'll have to hire someone to help." At another, "It won't be easy for him," and then, "He's hardworking, but writing out the bills, sales tax, feed prices—he can't handle that."

Karl knew he should really take her straight to Steiner, but he thought about the Long One's manner and decided to talk to her alone first.

At the station, he made coffee, and Hanna said, after trying it, "Your coffee's good, but if you put a little pinch of cinnamon in with the powder, it would be even better." She smiled, and Karl thought he had seldom seen her smile.

She put her cup down and, unprompted, began to talk.

When Hanna stepped out of the house to milk the cows, early in the morning of August 13, 1950, Therese was sitting on a bench behind the house. It was barely possible to speak to her. She kept saying, "I hit him and killed him." Hanna fetched her father, and Paul came too. It was almost an hour before Therese was able to give a more or less clear account of what had happened. Old Höver found out for the first time that Paul had seen Wilhelm and Theo Gerhard shoot Yuri. Paul stammered that he could not have known, at the time, that it was wrong. "There was a war on. Yuri was the enemy, after all," he said.

Höver struck Paul in the face, roaring that shooting unarmed enemies in the back was always wrong, even in wartime. Hanna was extremely worried that Therese might talk about her denunciation of Leonard too, but she did not mention it. Bit by bit, they learned that Wilhelm had come home, Therese had grabbed the poker and lashed out in the dark, and the iron had struck his companion, Friedhelm Lubisch. "Wilhelm's gone," she said. Her whole body was trembling, and she asked Hanna's father to come with her to the police station. "I was going to go myself, straight away, but I'm afraid. Theo Gerhard will be there again, like when I was arrested," she said, weeping.

Hanna's father asked Paul what Gerhard and Peters had done with Yuri's body, but all Paul knew was that they had dragged him to the car. In a whisper, Therese told them how Yuri's escape had come about, about Gerhard, who had shot a stranger, and her promise to marry Wilhelm. Old Höver sat in silence for a long time. His gaze wandered over the flat land, piercing hedges and fences, and landed on the horizon, where the first soft light of dawn was appearing. He stood up. "Enough deaths, enough misery," he said curtly. "Who does it help if you go to prison now?" He and Paul went to the cottage. The well had half collapsed during the war and was no longer in use. They wrapped the stranger in a blanket, threw him down the well, filled it in, and demolished the visible part of the stonework.

Hanna told her story fluently and almost without emotion. Occasionally she broke off, and a deep groove appeared between her eyebrows. Then she nodded briefly, as if confirming to herself what remained to be told. Her tone was steady, and Karl was certain she would not leave anything out, that she wanted to wipe the slate clean once and for all. "Therese stayed with us until Tuesday afternoon, and then she went to the police, as my father had told her, to report her husband missing. Theo Gerhard took over the investigation and, right from the start, accused Therese of having killed Wilhelm. He interrogated her for hours, shouting and threatening. At one point he whispered to her, 'Seven years ago you got away with it, you whore, but now you're going to get what you deserved back then.'"

A week later, Therese came to the farm and said Gerhard had ordered that the whole site where the cottage stood be turned upside down. Old Höver went to the town hall, as he had when Fedir was beaten up. Paul went with him. When they came back, he said to Therese in his taciturn way, "Don't worry about it."

The land was never searched. Gerhard maintained the outward appearance of the relentless investigator for a while, but he was cautious, and once Therese had gone, no more was heard from him.

Hanna got up, stood by the window, and stared out. "That Gerhard, he's still there. He gets a good pension and is a respectable citizen." Karl thought about Gerhard's blustering way of talking, the cognac in the morning, and the apartment he did not inhabit.

He spoke to Hanna's back. "Your father threatened to report him for shooting Yuri?" Hanna nodded. "In a sense, yes. I know from Paul that Father put the matter more simply. He just said, 'You shot two prisoners of war in the back. I know it, you know it, and now you should let things lie.'"

Karl offered her another coffee, but she stayed by the window and shook her head. He poured himself some more. "Have you been in contact with Therese Mende all along?" He saw Hanna start at the name. She said, "Yes, we've found out her current identity."

She turned to lean against the windowsill. "About two years after she left, a letter came from Frankfurt. She asked us to get her a copy of her birth certificate and take care of her parents' grave. From then on, there were regular Christmas letters with money for the care of the grave. They came from London, Paris, Amsterdam, and God knows where else. But there was never a return address—there was always just *Therese*. She didn't come and visit until just before Paul's wife died. I wasn't there. She came to the farm, and she was probably quite shocked at the way things looked. She offered to buy the cottage from Paul, but he had already leased it to the Albers woman because he was short of money. After that, she got in touch regularly. She tried to help Paul financially, but he was too proud, and probably he also felt guilty about her. At some point I mentioned that I could imagine setting up a boarding stable of some sort on the farm, and when Paul was widowed, she gave us the money to convert it and start the business."

Karl smiled. "The word here is that the money came from Paul's wife's life insurance."

Hanna laughed shortly. "We never said that, but you know what it's like in the village. If there's no official explanation, people just make one up. It suited us."

She looked down at the floor and fell silent. Karl stood beside her at the window. "Was there a condition attached to the money?" he asked softly.

"No. No condition. When we began making money with the horses, I wanted to pay her back in installments. She wouldn't accept it. These last years were the best for Paul and me, and then that Albers woman came and started stirring up the old stories."

Chapter 40

April 25, 1998

Robert Lubisch had drunk the second cognac. The remnants of the sun laid a purple path across the water, flaring up one last time. The perfect view struck him as inappropriate, and at the same time he felt the play of colors having a calming effect on his bewilderment. The cognac played its part too, burning in his throat and stomach and driving away the numbness in his body. Therese Mende fell silent, and there was a moment when he thought, *She's lying.*

But then his gaze returned to the photograph, and he admitted to himself that there was no doubt. He was Wilhelm Peters's son. He remembered a trip one Christmas at the beginning of the nineties. The borders were open, and he and his wife, Maren, had offered his father a trip to Wrocław, the former Breslau, as a gift. His father had not seemed pleased, and in the end his mother had gone there with a friend, supposedly because he could not be spared from the firm. And even when the Association of Displaced Persons, on whose board he sat, organized trips to the old homeland, he had never gone. He had said that a visit like that would reopen old wounds.

Luisa came and asked Therese Mende when and where she should serve dinner. Robert did not hear her answer. A short while later, Luisa brought wine and some water.

Seagulls glided by weightlessly, their plumage tinged pink in the evening light.

Therese told him about the help she received from the Hövers and about the well, and that she had left Kranenburg in December 1950.

He asked, "Did you ever make contact with him again?"

"No. I could probably have found him, but . . ." She hesitated. "I wanted to forget." She looked directly at him. "For the first two years, I spent my life on a tightrope, constantly ensuring I left no trace. I did a variety of jobs in Frankfurt—seamstress, administrative assistant, telephone operator—but whenever my employers became impatient about receiving my papers, I had to leave again. Then Hanna got me my birth certificate and, at last, I had an identity. My new life began with that. I was Therese Pohl again, and I used my maiden name to erase Therese Peters."

Robert took a sip of wine. "And my father erased Wilhelm Peters when he took Friedhelm Lubisch's papers." He reflected that his father had left most of his fortune to the Association of Displaced Persons. Had he identified with Friedhelm Lubisch's life as closely as that, or was it an attempt at restitution?

He thought about the big house, the statue of Diana in the garden, the grand parties. Everything about that life had always seemed to him too big and too loud—all of it false and overblown. And yet it had never occurred to him that the size and volume were there to hide something.

Cautiously, he asked, "You said you had talked about it with your husband. Do you think you would have been able to keep it hidden from him forever?"

Therese Mende did not answer for some time. Then she said quietly, "You're asking whether your mother might have known, aren't you?" He stood up, took a few steps, and sat down again.

"Yes, perhaps that's my question."

"I can't answer it for you," she said neutrally, and he was forcibly reminded of the dream in which his mother said to him, "You're destroying his life's work." Then she had gone away, and he was standing on the thread of her shawl and the stitches came unraveled, exposing his mother's back.

He felt the shock fading, felt himself beginning to look the truth in the eye, noticed that, for the first time, he was thinking, *My father, Wilhelm Peters.*

He stood up again and paced up and down. At length, he asked, "And Rita Albers? What happened to Rita Albers?"

"She called me," said Therese, and Robert noticed a change in tone. Her voice was steady; she had not had to cast back into the distant past. Now it was the businesswoman speaking, narrating the facts succinctly and precisely.

"I knew from Paul Höver that she had a picture of me and was asking questions. She called me, and I threatened her over the phone, but it was clear to me that she wasn't going to be stopped that way. I called a friend in Frankfurt, a lawyer, the same day and asked him to offer her money."

She paused, got up, and went to stand by the balustrade. "'A big story,' she had said, and that meant she wanted to sell it for a high price."

She went over to the table and picked up her glass of white wine. "My lawyer was unable to reach her, and the next day I heard from Hanna Höver that she had been found dead." This too she said in the most matter-of-fact way. She twirled the glass in her hands, and the heavy wine slid viscously up the side of the glass, refracting the evening light. "Although I knew better, I hoped that would be the end of the story." She looked at Robert Lubisch and smiled mirthlessly. "And then you came, and when I saw you, I knew the time had finally come. I'll tell you frankly that I didn't decide to tell you the truth about that night in the summer of 1950 until this morning." She pointed at the leather wallet that contained the wedding photograph. "Even if I were to destroy it, what would happen if my daughter, like you, went on the hunt after my death? She assumes I grew up in the lower Rhine, that my parents died in the war, and that I married her father in 1956. She's never been to Kranenburg, doesn't question my past. What if she wants more detail one day? Whose truth will she get to hear?" She turned around and looked out to sea, where the line of the horizon now clearly separated the sky and the water. Robert Lubisch stood beside her. Quietly she said, "Do you think the truth would have been easier to bear if you had heard it from your father?"

Time piled up on the tiled floor behind them; the day had definitively given up its place. Robert spoke toward the sea. His words dropped down the slope. "What hurts the most is that those intimate moments alone with him in his study, when he told me about his family, his escape, and his captivity, were among the best moments of my childhood." He laughed bitterly. "It's hard to accept that we were at our closest when he was lying to me."

Therese Mende listened to him attentively, watched the lights go on one by one in the hotels, restaurants, and bars, and tried to reassure herself with the thought that she had kept part of her life secret from her daughter, but had never presented her with a stranger's life. Robert too was lost in thought. He felt tears coming into his eyes and drove them off by breathing hard. Then he said, "When my father died, I mourned him. Just now, I felt as if he were dying again, but that's not true. He doesn't exist. Even his tombstone is a lie now."

Chapter 41

April 25, 1998

Hanna had sat down in the chair in front of Karl van den Boom's desk. Deep in thought, she was plucking at the big white bow at her breast, which seemed to bother her. She was not comfortable in her skirt either, and kept smoothing it down. Karl reflected that she looked as if she were in fancy dress.

"First, that Albers woman came to the farm with the photo. She acted innocent, wanted to know what had become of Therese, if we knew anything about her. She had already been to old Heuer, claimed to have Therese's name from him."

Karl rumbled his understanding, but did not say a word to interrupt Hanna. He thought about her sparing, monosyllabic way with words. Today, it seemed to him, she was using up a year's worth of words.

"I called Therese, told her she was sniffing about." Her work-hardened hands were scuffing the finely woven fabric of her shawl, pulling little threads loose. She noticed and put her hands in her lap. Her eyes wandered restlessly over the desk. Then she stopped and looked at him. "On the television they always have some kind of recording machine. Don't you need one?" Karl pursed his lips and shook his head. "You'll have to say all this again to my colleagues in Kalkar," he said evenly, and she looked at him suspiciously. "But I won't do that," she said decisively, her voice firm. He held up his hand soothingly. "I suggest you finish your story first, and then we'll see what's to be done." Her broad forehead creased in a frown, and then she seemed to agree.

"Good. So, I thought . . . they won't get much out of us if we don't say anything. What can they find anyway? But you get to thinking, don't you, and . . ." Her hands seemed to be fighting each other in her lap. "Paul inherited the farm because . . . well, he was the son. He hadn't had an easy life, and I . . . I had promised Father I would take care of the farm and Paul. But when Sofia came . . . we didn't get along, and then I went away too. Sofia was no farmer, and Paul, he's a hard worker, but he needs someone to tell him what to do. When the market for milk went down, everyone else switched over to pigs, and Paul just kept going, hoping it would get better someday. But it didn't, and then he leased or sold the land. He didn't think far enough ahead to realize he wouldn't be able to grow feed for the cattle anymore and would have to buy it at a high price . . . He shouldn't have been allowed to lease out the cottage, but Sofia didn't understand why, and of course he couldn't explain, so he just did it." Hanna had tears in her eyes now. She picked up her handbag, which she had placed on the floor, and took out a carefully ironed handkerchief. Embarrassed, she wiped her eyes. Karl was moved to see the surly Hanna in such a vulnerable state. She lowered her head in embarrassment, avoiding his gaze.

"I thought, if Paul has to go to jail because of what he and Father did with the stranger all that time ago . . . he won't survive. Not him." She sucked air into her lungs and, as she breathed out slowly, shook her head resignedly. "I thought perhaps we'd be spared that, but then Schoofs called, asking about the well. Then I knew she'd found out." She unfolded the handkerchief and blew her nose loudly. "I couldn't sleep that night. I got up around midnight and looked out of the window. There was still a light on in the cottage. I thought Paul had given her the lease on the place for a ridiculously low rent, and for thanks she was sending him to the slaughter. I was so furious." She raised her head and stared past Karl at the wall, as if she might be able to find that evening there.

She got dressed and left the farmhouse; she wanted to think it over in the fresh air, what was to be done now. Then she was on the path through the fields. It was pitch-dark. She stopped, searched for sentences, words with which she could stop Rita Albers, but what could she say? All she could think of were empty threats.

Moving on, she stumbled over a tussock of grass, fell down, and was overcome by an intolerable feeling of helplessness as she lay on the ground. From the road in the distance, the white light of a pair of headlights wandered across the night, and the sound of an engine died away. She struggled to her feet and went on, closer and closer to the brightly lit cottage, driven by a red heat within her that seemed to scream, *Make her keep silent.*

She entered the property through the garden, saw that the terrace door was open, and went in. Rita Albers was sitting at the kitchen table when she stopped in the corridor. Rita did not notice her. She was absorbed in the papers that lay spread out over the table. Hanna saw the heading "Mende Fashion" on one of the sheets of paper.

The red heat in her head exploded.

She looked at Karl van den Boom, and now her hands lay still in her lap. "And then I had her meat hammer in my hand and she was lying with her head on the table among the papers. Then there was peace." She said this with a childlike surprise, and after a short pause she added matter-of-factly, "I took the hammer and the folder with the papers outside with me. Her rubber gloves were lying on the table on the terrace. I thought, if it looks like a break-in . . . I put the gloves on, scattered the papers over the floor, smashed the vase against the ground, and took the laptop away." She lowered her head in shame.

Karl stood up, went to the window, and lost himself in the young greenness of the linden tree. He considered whether he should tell Hanna that Rita Albers knew nothing about the well. That Schoofs had only wanted to know how deep he would need to drill for the new well.

He remained silent.

Epilogue

The remains of Friedhelm Lubisch, deceased in 1950, were buried in the cemetery at Kranenburg on May 7, 1998.

When Hanna found out that Paul's crime—the disposal of Friedhelm Lubisch's body—was long since statute-barred, she broke down. She spent the time leading up to her trial at the Höver farm. Therese Mende posted her bail. In the fall of 1999, Hanna was given a three-year prison sentence, of which she served two years. In 2007, at age eighty-six, she died on the farm.

Therese Mende was able to talk to her daughter before the press pounced on the case. Her lawyers made skillful tactical use of petitions and identified various procedural errors. She died in 2002 at her house in Mallorca, before the case went to trial.

Robert Lubisch did not have the name on his father's grave changed. In 1999, he donated his entire inheritance to a charitable foundation.

Paul leased the boarding stables to a trainer with a family. He retains a lifelong right to live on the property and now dedicates himself to his vegetable garden.

CHARACTERS

THEN:

The childhood friends:

Therese Pohl	*born 1922*
Leonard Kramer	*born 1921*
Hanna Höver	*born 1921*
Jacob Kalder	*born 1920*
Alwine Kalder	*born 1922*
Wilhelm Peters	*born 1920*

Siegmund Pohl	*Doctor, Therese Pohl's father*
Margarete Pohl	*Therese Pohl's mother*
Gustav Höver	*Farmer, Hanna and Paul Höver's father*
August Hollmann	*Captain in the SS*

1998:

Robert Lubisch	*Doctor, Friedhelm Lubisch's son*
Rita Albers	*Journalist*
Karl van den Boom	*Police sergeant*
Manfred Steiner	*Police chief inspector, Homicide*
Brand	*Police inspector, Homicide*
Theo Gerhard	*Retired police sergeant*
Thomas Köbler	*Journalist, friend of Rita Albers*
Tillmann and Therese Mende	*Entrepreneurs*

ABOUT THE AUTHOR

Born in 1960, Mechtild Borrmann lives in Bielefeld, Germany. She spent her childhood and youth in the lower Rhine region—the setting for her crime stories. She works as a dance and theater instructor, among other professions. She is the author of *Morgen ist der Tag nach Gestern* (*Tomorrow Is the Day After Yesterday*, 2007) and *Mitten in der Stadt* (*Right in the City*, 2009). *Silence* (*Wer das Schweigen bricht*) won the 2012 Deutscher Krimi Prize for best crime novel, and it marks her English debut.

ABOUT THE TRANSLATOR

Aubrey Botsford has previously translated Katia Fox's *The Silver Falcon* and *The Golden Throne*, as well as novels by Yasmina Khadra and Enrico Remmert. He lives in London.